THE DEATH OF LYSANDA

OTHER WORKS IN DALKEY ARCHIVE PRESS'S
HEBREW LITERATURE SERIES

Dolly City
Orly Castel-Bloom

Heatwave and Crazy Birds
Gabriela Avigur-Rotem

Homesick
Eshkol Nevo

Kin
Dror Burstein

Life on Sandpaper
Yoram Kaniuk

Motti
Asaf Schurr

THE DEATH
OF
LYSANDA

Two Novellas

YITZHAK ORPAZ

TRANSLATED BY RICHARD FLINT AND DAVID ZARAF
Series Editor: Rachel S. Harris

DALKEY ARCHIVE PRESS
CHAMPAIGN / LONDON / DUBLIN

The Death of Lysanda was originally published in Hebrew as *Mot Lysanda* by Sifriat Poalim Ltd, Jerusalem, 1964; *Ants* was originally published in Hebrew as *Nemalim* by Am Oved, Tel Aviv, 1968

Richard Flint's translation of *The Death of Lysanda* first published by Jonathan Cape, London, 1970; David Zaraf's translation of *Ants* first appeared in *The Iowa Review*, 1980

Library of Congress Cataloging-in-Publication data is available

Partially funded by a grant from the Illinois Arts Council, a state agency

The Hebrew Literature Series is published in collaboration with the Institute for the Translation of Hebrew Literature and sponsored by the Office of Cultural Affairs, Consulate General of Israel in New York

www.dalkeyarchive.com

Printed on permanent/durable acid-free paper and bound in the United States of America

Cover: design and composition by Nicholas Motte

Contents

THE DEATH
OF
LYSANDA
TRANSLATED BY RICHARD FLINT

Editor's Note

The pages that follow were written by Naphtali Noi himself. They were discovered in a prison cell by one of my acquaintances, a policeman, who, thinking they would interest me, passed them on.

They did interest me. I felt they had to be published.

For the convenience of the reader, I have edited and arranged the pages in a reasonable sequence, retaining almost all of their contents.

I have tried to preserve, as much as is possible, the tone of the original. And it is for the reader to judge.

I

I fixed myself a light meal in the kitchen. It was already two o'clock in the morning—the time I usually come home from the newspaper, where I work as a proofreader, and fix myself a light meal. I was tired and wanted to sleep. I would have fallen on my bed and gone straight to sleep, but I was so tired that I did not have the strength to go against habit. My hands did what they had done so many nights, and I found myself leaning over the small kitchen cupboard, with tea and cheese sandwiches in front of me, and an old newspaper spread out under them.

I was very tired, but as I saw characters I glanced over them to seek out a missing *i* or a superfluous *e*—inevitable for a proofreader—and my eyes fell on two items. The first was an advertisement for a film, in which He and She featured; "She, wicked and corrupt from birth," (here I was annoyed by the use of a comma instead of a colon) "an illegitimate child." "He: a tempestuous playboy driven out of his mind by youthful passion." And both of them "like Adam and Eve in the Garden of Eden, naked and unashamed." The final sentence was printed entirely in Gothic script. Underneath this advertisement was a news item about a man who had killed his wife and told his interrogators: "I had a headache and couldn't sleep all night. I got up in the morning and wandered around the yard. I saw a big rock. I picked it up and dropped it on my wife's head."

The wife's name was Eve. I was taken by the clear, restrained, almost classical style of this paragraph.

The window in front of me was open and I really do not know why it bothered me. Anyhow, I grabbed it and shook it, trying to close it, before taking the tea in my hand. I was still new on the roof of this old house—I had not been here for more than four weeks—and I was not yet accustomed to all its nooks and crannies. In any case, the window frame, after hitting against the sill, opened up again, dragging with it the other frame. I threw my hand forward to stop it so that the pane would not smash into the corner of the shelf, but before I could reach it I knocked over the cup of tea. The tea spilled out, the cup broke, and I looked around me and saw that it was night. Deepest night. And the wind whistling through the window and the window wide open.

I went out on to the roof. The roof was square, but the darkness was thick, and I could not see its corners. And the trees that always lined the street below were also invisible. As I could not see the corners of the roof, I did not see the plants I raised and nurtured so diligently in the corners of the roof. I heard only a kind of rustle from them, something like a frightened breathing. Then a wind came and cast a feverish tingling over the roof. It wound around like a black flame. Perhaps I felt that a more powerful wind was following—anyway I went into my room and fell on my face. I lay there, feeling on my back and on my neck that all the doors and all the windows had burst wide open.

I opened an eye—and from then on I lay, one eye closed and one eye open.

II

Before Naphtali Noi came to this city he had been married to a girl from an Orthodox family in Jerusalem. Her name was Leah. The marriage had lasted four years ("Just like a pair of doves, you never hear them coming in or going out," the neighbors had said) and they had no children.

In the mornings Naphtali used to work in the archives of one of the museums of which Jerusalem is so full, and in the afternoons he would study in their quiet apartment, jotting down notes, while Leah walked on tiptoe so as not to disturb his work. From time to time he would go out with his friend Peretz to the Judean Hills, where they would hunt wild duck and hedgehogs and bring the meat home. Leah couldn't stand it and Naphtali had to eat it alone.

One day he dragged home a skinned hedgehog, stuck by its blood to a filthy sack, and found Leah vomiting, laughing through her tears and saying, "There's a child in my womb. There's a child in my womb." Naphtali refused to believe this, but he saw that his wife's stomach was swollen. He washed the blood off his hands, began feeling her stomach, and with a trembling hand pulled out from under her dress the feather pillow that she always loved to clasp in her lap. And Leah laughed through her tears—slowly the tears overwhelmed the laughter, "I told you, I told you there's a child in my womb, but you don't believe me, you don't believe me." Naphtali went up to the roof of the house and looked out at the steeples and domes of the churches of which Jerusalem is so full.

Then he took up taxidermy.

From Jerusalem Naphtali set out for any high mountain peak. And on one of these, near Kibbutz Omrah in Galilee, he met Sternik, who used to stuff birds and small animals and sell them.

Sternik was proud of his craft and strict about its rules. He taught Naphtali patience in operating on a dead animal. "Smoke a pipe—it's food for patience," he said. Naphtali started smoking a pipe. But with all the rest he was not so successful. Sternik taught him how to draw out the blood gradually, how to clean off the dirt with various solutions and how to write out a kind of identity card for the dead animal, with personal details like total length, weight, wingspan, sex, color of eyes, length of beak, contents of stomach, and so on. Then how to move the wings of the carcass from side to side to render them flexible before the operation.

"The operation," explained Sternik, "mainly consists of turning the bird inside out as one does a glove, in the process amputating, step by step, only those parts whose amputation allows the maximum preservation of the skin in its entirety. Thus, the eyes are thrown away and their color noted, the brain is thrown away and the skull retained, and the skin is carefully cleaned of fat. Then—and only then—the skin is to be turned (again—like a glove) back, to be given the appearance of a living creature by means of joining and stuffing." Naphtali was a good listener, but a poor pupil. Sternik taught him to respect the creatures and to set them up after the operation in their normal position, that which was most natural to them. Not in the manner of some "charlatans" ("some have made it into even this respected craft")—who set up a bird with one wing raised and a foot tensed, as if poised for flight, with its beak open, ready to screech.

It seems that Naphtali did not quite understand Sternik. He tired very quickly of all rules. Instead of soft, flexible wire, he used springy steel, and instead of sawdust that had been specially imported from abroad, he stuffed seaweed into the open bellies. Nor did he observe the precise sequence of steps of the operation. But what particularly aroused his fastidious teacher's ire was Naphtali's style—his style of setting up the bird. Naphtali found no respect whatever, in himself, for the "normal" stance of a creature; he saw no heresy in a bird tensing for flight. On the contrary, the normal, natural pose of the creature annoyed him. His eyes rolled, his pipe clattered between his teeth. In a state of elation he would lengthen the short neck of the thrush, bend the straight beak of the kingfisher, shorten the legs of the hawk, tear off the feathers and stick round, owl-like eyes into the head of the pigeon. Actually he aimed at greater and more terrible distortions than these, but Sternik's professional strictness kept him in check. Who was Naphtali Noi quarrelling with? He had left Jerusalem and his wife, had stopped eating meat, but went on killing the creatures of the Creator. What for? To give them a new form.

"There are already quite enough charlatans in this profession," said Sternik one day and sent him away from his workshop.

And Naphtali Noi came to live on a rooftop in this city and went on with his work. He tried to sell some of his stuffed birds and was glad he could not find any buyers. There was nothing like them in the biology books. Naphtali went to work as a proofreader. He would spend the evenings at the newspaper and the mornings on his own work. And the hour between day and night he would spend on neither of these, but would stand silent—the pipe in his mouth upside down and extinguished—and stare in turn at the houses of the city, the sea, and the fringes of the sky.

III

The geranium is a modest plant; it stays in its place, withdrawn, does not spread out unduly, does not demand much water or manure, and yet gives out flowers all year round. And the flowers too are modest, tiny, pale blue or red in color, and when they wither they fall into the box and fertilize the plant. I just have to pass my hand over them, and a great tranquility flows into it—and then into me.

A horrible voice, a woman's voice: "Don't go, I told you. No. It'll be the end of you, I said. The end of you." The voice was swallowed up in the crying of a child or perhaps of a number of children; the voice broke up into many voices. In the house next door was a huge, closed window. There, I thought, the voices break. In the room stood a heavy table with four wooden legs and the table was covered with a white tablecloth on which was a two-branched silver candlestick with lighted candles. This table was amazingly similar to the dining table in my grandfather's house when I was a child. I had never seen a living person beside this table. I threw a stone at the window and it seemed to sink into clay or sand, without sound and without echo.

I went up to the edge of the roof, looking with all my eyes. The same ancient, heavy table. And the candles, alight. No. There was no one there. The sea glinted beyond the roof. Not the big sea, just a thin strip of sea, preparing itself for the sun. In another two or three hours the sun would come into it and it would cover itself with gloom, and a shadow would steal into my heart from there. I opened the box in which I kept all my various taxidermy materials: seaweed, scissors, nylon thread, plastic glue, plastic paints, wire, and some iron implements. I took a hammer and some small steel nails and went down to the entrance of the house to put up my mailbox.

Naphtali was known in intellectual circles as a person of original taste, a man of knowledge. And since no one could say exactly in which field he was most talented, he was sent periodicals and journals of all kinds from the Bible Society, the Society for the Preservation of Flora, and the Society for Moral Improvement, was sent archaeological, philological, literary, and astrological reviews—and was urged to express an opinion on this or that and, if possible, to contribute an article of his own.

It's worth noting that, although many people had heard of Naphtali Noi, very few had met him, and of these very few, very few indeed were among his acquaintances. It would not be correct to say that people turned away from him. There were also those who were very happy to exchange a word or two with him. There was something hearty in his big brown eyes. His face was full, even sated. He was squat and solid in stature. His walk was easy, and his smile unexpected. He could send out a smile from any part of his face. This smile was perhaps pleasant to see, but it was very private, and generally did not encourage people to approach him and speak to him. His acquaintances knew that this smile of his was not meant for them, and so they remained within their own borders and Naphtali in his.

Because they left him on his own, he did not turn them down nor did he deny his own impulses, and so from time to time he would send an article to one journal or another. "The Eclipse of the Moon and the Eclipse of the Mind," "Archaeology and the Loss of Purpose in Modern Existence," "The Use of the Name of God and the Magic of the Word," "From the Machine Age to the Age of Silence," "The Revolt of the Beautiful in Nature," and so on. The articles called up echoes and sharp retorts from one circle or another and soon sank into an oblivion of stalemate. And Naphtali Noi, rather than being astonished at the short lives of his articles, would wonder at the fuss they caused in this or that academic circle; his eyes would pucker up and his smile would sink dimples in his full cheeks. Dark dimples.

When I came to live in this house I put my mailbox up in the downstairs entrance. The next day I found it hanging about forty centimeters higher than I had left it. There was a note in the aperture: "We have moved your mailbox so that it will not prevent access to the light switch for the stairs at night. Thanking you, the Tenants of the House." In my imagination I saw all the tenants of the house holding the mailbox at once, pulling it down with one pull, and with the pounding of tens of hands fixing it in its new place. It also annoyed me that in order to remove the box from its original place and put it up in its new one, they would have had to open it, for the nails had been banged into the wall from inside the box. Which meant that the tenants of the house supposed that my mailbox was communal property. I put the box back in its original place. The next day I found it higher up again, this time with no note. I put it back in its place again.

So my mailbox changed places all the time. It should be said, to the credit of the tenants, that they never disturbed me in my work when I came down to repair what they had spoiled. But as time went by the nail holes in the box got too wide and I had to make new ones. And the holes in the wall multiplied, till I was forced to use longer nails. My only consolation was that my neighbors were forced to do the same.

I had not eaten since morning and the work of putting up the mailbox had increased my hunger. I washed my hands and face and headed for the kitchen to eat something. The doorbell rang, and a bearded man with a pleasant, comfortable, but slightly bewildered face was standing in the doorway. He asked if Naphtali Noi lived here. I said to him, "No, what do you mean, there's no Naphtali Noi here, and actually there's no Naphtali Noi at all." But I was all upset about nothing, because the man was quiet, modest, and didn't really seem like he meant to do me any harm. And, anyhow, he wasn't looking at me but at my taxidermy. There was something undefined in his eyes: a question, or a warning. When he saw that I was annoyed he turned and went.

Even as he was going he didn't scold or shout at me. He just said, "You're Naphtali Noi. I only wanted to see. I'll come some other time." He even looked familiar to me—he resembled that bearded character who sells combs in the city streets. That one's flesh weeps through his rags and this one was properly dressed, other than that they only differed in dress. I actually expected him to pull out a pile of multicolored combs from his pocket and offer them to me. The one in the street would add, at times, in between combs, a kind of warning: "The last train is leaving, gentlemen! The last train is leaving!" I bet his train had already left many years ago. Somehow I was pleased when he told me he would come again to have a look at my stuffed animals.

I was lost in thought when the door to the roof burst open like in a whirlwind and my two little angels, the twins Nili and Lili, fell upon me.

The noise Nili and Lili are capable of making could fill a king's palace, let alone a miserable space like mine. At first they walk contentedly on either side of me, casting long glances at the stuffed wildfowl, staring at each other, and then their fluttering eyes begin to smile. I've never been able to understand how the circles of their eyes can contain so much light. Their faces change shades, like a strip of sea being played with by the sun.

"Why is his head so high?"

"So he can see a long way," I answered.

"And can he fly?"

"No," I said.

"So why can't he fly?"

"Because he's got straw in his belly."

"But why has he got straw in his belly?"

"So he can't fly."

Nili's eyes grew very wide and darkened a little. Lili did not hear. She only looked on.

"So why is he looking up so high?"

And then, in unison, as though a hidden signal had been received, the two began to fly around the roof with their little skirts waving. And Naphtali ran after them afraid that their feet might leave the roof and they might take wing. He did not catch them, but they caught him.

They are playing catch with him. One pulls his trousers, and as he rolls after her to catch her the other one pinches him there, and he runs after her. And the voices of both chime out, and their peals of laughter resound on the roof like golden bells. By this time Naphtali is already down on all fours and feeling like a wildcat, a kind of cheetah, or a young tiger pouncing on a pair of gazelles. And then the hoarse and dangerous trumpet of the hunter is heard:

"Ni-li-li! Li-li-li! The soup's getting cold!" This is Mrs. Schturz, the mother of the twins, a woman of great girth and with a strong but hoarse voice. It's a wonder how such a coarse voice can put together two such delicate-sounding names. "Ni-li-li!" the voice calls. Naphtali straightens up and shakes his trousers, and the little ones open their eyes wide and listen. Actually the roof is dirty. Between the flowerpots and ferns strips of wall stare out, peeled of their plaster. Blobs of black tar are stuck in little piles all over the roof. Like an old patched-up garment.

"Nililili! The soup's getting cold—Father's waiting—"

Nili and Lili gather their wings and next to the door the two of them say in unison:

"Mama said you should come at four o'clock."

Their mother, Mrs. Schturz, a large-limbed flushed-faced housewife, did not particularly like me, but she was on to a good thing with me, since I would entertain the twins whenever she went to town. She herself never bothered me, so she didn't owe me any thanks. It was enough for me to hear Nili and Lili chirp.

If Mrs. Schturz didn't particularly like me, Mr. Schturz did not particularly hate me. I didn't really know him, as I didn't really know the other tenants of the house, but this I did know, that whenever I was called down to their flat—he was not at home. Once when I was going down there he passed or crept by me like a shadow, and if you can believe that a shadow can say hello, then Mr. Schturz said hello to me. The house is old, the windows of the staircase are blocked with bricks and sandbags from the days of war, and on the staircase of the house a man looks like a shadow.

The sun entered into a thick cloud, a remnant of the winter, as into a hairy coat, and this tickled my kidneys. Of the lilting laughter of the little ones nothing remained but rags interspersed with nervous silence. The palpitations of my heart seeped down into my stomach. I went into the bathroom. There is a wide drainpipe there that goes from ceiling to floor, then down into the Schturz's apartment, from there into the lower floors of the house, and from there joins a wider pipe that continues under the ground and on to a pipe that is wider still, and so on. It is a wonderful conductor of sound. I closed the window so that the noises from outside wouldn't disturb me, and caught a glimpse of my face in the mirror. Burning eyes turned away from me. I ignored them and looked around. There was no one there with me.

Naphtali sat down on the step of his shower stall, turned his face inside and pressed his head to the pipe.

IV

No one but me knows Lysanda. And the reason is simple—I created her.

God created man from dust and Eve from his rib; I made Lysanda as I rocked alone in my rocking chair on long, lonely evenings. And I didn't make her all at once.

My mother, may she rest in peace, was a beautiful woman. But I could not bear the flesh of her arm. It was thick, and flopped a bit when she moved her hand to pat my head, and even more when she moved it to hit me. My first love would set off my masculinity with her wide-open eyes. Then those open eyes would melt me and I could do nothing to close them. I re-invented Lysanda continually, according to my needs.

Her hair, the color of smoldering embers, falls smoothly around her shoulders. Her shoulders are like two slightly raised mounds of ivory, one a little higher than the other (why?—I wanted it that way), and a sliver of shadow falls from them and tapers, warm and flickering, between her breasts. Her eyes are calm and good, and her eyebrows are raised questioningly. Her chin is made to support the entire range of smiles I need, as the occasion requires, without adding to them or detracting from them.

Her appearance: a sea that has suddenly frozen—a sea of stillness and motion.

In the beginning she wore red sandals on her feet, and she would float above the roof. I said to her, "Come down and stand on the roof." She came down a little, but her sandals still didn't touch the roof. I made her white sandals and said to her, "Come down and stand on the roof." She refused and said, "The white will get dirty on the roof." I made her gray sandals. What did she do? She threw the sandals away and came down on to the roof in her bare feet, smiling at me. Perhaps she did this to demonstrate a degree of independence. Anyhow, I stared at her with angry loving eyes.

She had wonderful hands. One day she came to me wearing dark gloves. I almost threw her out. She giggled, and the gloves faded away like a shadow. Perhaps like the shadow in my heart.

Before I married Leah everyone was sure I would marry Anath. Anath was very pretty—the prettiest girl I've ever seen. Her mother told me, "You're getting a treasure, make sure you know how to keep it." I understood she wasn't exaggerating. Leah wasn't pretty, she was even a bit ugly. But her great suffering had spun a fine thread of grace across her face. When sorrow came upon her, she would close her shutters on the world for a day or two. There were thick books of suffering in her heart, and at times I would help her leaf through them.

That evening I had to decide between their two houses—and in both of them they were waiting for me. I can't say this didn't please me—to be the one waited for, the one with the choice in his hands. I should add that for a long time I had done all I could to make sure that the decision—which meanwhile I had postponed again and again—should remain my sole prerogative. And when the time came, and they were waiting for me in both their houses, in both houses on the same day and at the same time—whose house should I go to? Anath was the paragon of all virtues. Her beauty alone was enough to set me trembling. Nor did she lack understanding, status, wealth, manners, graces.

It was a rainy evening and I was wearing my best clothes. I was close to the street where Anath lived. I could see the house with its glass-enclosed verandas. Currents of water swirled along the street, lapping up against the curb. I thought of my new shoes. It would be a pity to ruin them—they would probably get soaked as I crossed the street. I couldn't walk into Anath's elegant home, where her fastidious parents were waiting for me, in slimy shoes. I took a shortcut through a side street, and suddenly found myself outside the window of Leah's tiny room.

I made Lysanda just as I wanted her. And no water threatened to soak my shoes.

V

When Batia first came to him, she surprised him in the toilet. He was seated leaning over that drainpipe, listening to the familiar sounds from the Schturz apartment, for example, the measured steps of Mrs. Schturz leaving the house, or the sweet twitterings of Nili and Lili calling him to come down. He sat on the stone step of the shower, sweating, tense, disheveled, his face aglow. No, it wasn't exactly a position he liked to be seen in. She was big and preposterous; so big that if he had known some magic phrase that could have whisked this strange woman away, out of his sight, then—well it's doubtful he would have spoken it.

For, apart from the fact that she was not entirely alien—there was a book in her hand, one of his, he believed—she carried her high bosom, in its gray wool sweater, with pride, and her smile took in her protruding, determined chin and illuminated her tiny, gleaming teeth, which were rooted there like an inexorable statement.

Naphtali, slightly confused now, set his hands to work. He ran one down the drainpipe, picked up a few things, opened a tap and closed it. It was impossible to move. The woman was everywhere. He raised his head to the window and said that he had lost something and that he was looking for the something he had lost.

The visitor collected her smile and asked what he had lost. But Naphtali walked quickly out onto the roof, where he met the sun in the sky, and this dispelled his confusion. The woman's eyes were big, brown, and protuberant. He had a distinct feeling that if she was to get angry or excited, or if she fell in love, the eyes would leap out of their sockets. This disturbed him. She was also slightly, very slightly, cock-eyed—though in such a way that her gaze didn't wander out to the sides but closed in on whatever she saw. It was this—as he discovered later—that was largely responsible for the fact that in anger she looked absolutely furious; in pity, like the Mother of the Savior; in happiness, gleeful; and in sorrow, as though about to commit suicide. Her blonde hair was cut short, her nose and ears were small and neutral.

He said, "Sit down." She said, "Thank you, here's the book," and went to the edge of the roof to look out at the sea. I saw that her thighs were broad, almost bursting out of her narrow skirt, and the joints of her knees looked warm. I walked up to the bougainvillea, holding a pair of pruning shears. Lysanda stood facing me, smiling. I ignored her and looked at my watch. Five to four. And at four I had to be with my little ones.

Batia said, "You've got a nice roof." I said, "Yes," and she walked quickly up to the stuffed wildfowl and let out a "Hey" of surprise and said, "It's practically alive, and you don't even have to feed it." "You don't have to feed it," I said, "because it's full of straw." She laughed and exchanged glances with its tiny, glinting eyes. The wild bird's head was mounted on its long neck in such a way that while the left eye looked downward, the right one looked up at the sky.

With her finger she prodded a sharp, resilient feather that jutted out of its tail and said, "I wish I had one like it." "What next," I said to Lysanda, "What next." Lysanda said, "What next." Batia said, "Thanks, I knew you wouldn't turn me down," and hurried to the banister of the roof where she looked down and said, "You can get dizzy up here." Then she said, "It's wonderful to live on a roof," and shook her head, and with the book that was in her hand described a circle across the sky, and I saw there was something attractive about her forehead.

Batia spoke about Buki and said that she was sick of his stories. When she's alone in a room, she often wants the ceiling to vanish and the sky to lean down to her. "It's so near the sky here," she said. "Near enough to make you dizzy," I said. The plants had bowed their heads and shrunk, and the bougainvillea had donned a sad olive color over its gay blooms. All the lizards had disappeared from the roof. I got angry and said, "Enough to make you dizzy."

I looked at the door to the roof. It was open. It had been open when Batia invaded the place. My little ones, Nili and Lili, had left it open when they left and I had not closed it so I could hear the sounds of their little feet.

Batia didn't look at the door; she laughed. Already I felt that her skin was very thick, and though her laugh reverberated all over the roof, her skin didn't breathe at all.

She looked at the pavement and said that from up here you can't see the sweat and dirt. She sometimes dreams, she said, that she's up somewhere high, and she sees people as small as cats. "Like mechanized dolls," I said. "Like poor little mice," she said. "Like poor little cockroaches," I said. "Like mechanized cockroaches," she said. I agreed with her and she agreed with me and at that moment we saw that the world was a shameful world and her tiny hand rested miserable and helpless on my arm.

Yes, her hand was tiny, completely out of proportion to her big head, her firm chin, her short neck, her broad thighs and her breasts which were also resting on me, and not only on me, but on all the roof in all their abundance. The sleeves of her sweater were rolled up to the elbows and the skin of her arm was covered with a fine, pale down, like the skin of my mother's arm, may she rest in peace.

"Come on, Yakoko," rang the voices of the little ones downstairs. They called me "Yakoko." It was a sign of their affection. "Yakoko" was the Srulik's nickname, he was the son of the news vendor on the corner. He wears a cloth hat on his head winter and summer, and makes funny faces for the girls. Actually he makes faces at everyone, and no one can guess his age. A wave of sweetness spread through my stomach. I looked at my watch. It was half past four. Batia went inside the room and I went in after her. She rummaged around my books and said that Kierkegaard is a good writer and it's obvious that he suffered a lot and stuff because he loved Regina. I said to her that he had loved not Regina but through Regina. "What do you care if I love you," he had said. Batia stood up, faced me, pursed her lips almost painfully and called out, "No. He loved her and that's why he was so miserable." I said to her that Kierkegaard said that love consumes the lovers. She narrowed her gaze on me in anger and contempt, and the corners of her lips drooped down in disgust and she was unable to say a word. Then she moved away and fled to the window.

I said to her, "See that other window down there?" She said, "Yes." I said, "See the table with the white tablecloth with two candlesticks on it and two lit candles in them?" She said, "I can't see a thing except an old, boring, musty room," and turned around to straighten the pictures on my wall. Then I said, to pacify her, "What I meant to say to you before was that Kierkegaard is a cry to God."

Batia sat down on the bed, serious, her lips pursed, her chin firm, her eyes frozen. I should have offered her some coffee, but it was already half past four, and at half past five Mrs. Schturz comes back home and receives visitors and the little girls chirp and call, "Yakoko, come on down!" I sat in a chair opposite her, and Batia started to speak and said that there is a kind of sadness in the house and all at once she feels that here thought is superfluous. Her big bosom rose and fell as she said that she gets terribly frightened when, at times, she feels this way, as if she were losing her common sense. I said, "Perhaps it's because there isn't enough light in the room," and offered to turn on the light. "No," she said, rummaged in her handbag, took out a cigarette, lit a match with a trembling hand, and said that the smoke of the cigarette gives her back her common sense. I brought an ashtray and said that even common sense doesn't always make sense. And Naphtali Noi sat next to her, held her free hand in his, and laughed into his liver as he told her the story about Peretz and the rooster.

Peretz and Naphtali used to go hunting together. Peretz was a he-man type, with big hands, a dirty mouth, and the strength of an ox. There was nothing false about him, and as a result everybody liked him and he liked everybody. Peretz loved three things—a good hunt, a hearty meal, and a healthy woman with meat on her bones.

One day they went hunting near Nahal Reuven and caught nothing but a few marsh birds. It was raining, and they wallowed in mud and were as hungry as wolves. They came to the game warden's hut and held a council. Marsh birds cook very slowly and one can die of hunger before they're ready to eat. Peretz winked, went out, wandered to and fro, crowed a few times, and came back holding a handsome rooster, rich of plume, plump of breast, with a comb that stood erect like the crown of a king.

A spirit of fun came over Peretz, and instead of cutting the rooster's head off with one swing of a knife, in the usual way, this is what he did: He took his scout's knife out of its sheath and wiped it on his handkerchief. Then he looked at it in the dim light two or three times, like a professional butcher, to make sure the blade was sharp and smooth and flawless. Then he gathered the rooster's wings to its back and held them in one hand, pulled back the crowned head of the bird and blew into the feathers of its neck very religiously till he had cleared a space, mumbled something resembling a blessing and with his other hand passed the blade of the knife over the rooster's neck. Then he threw the rooster out into the rain to wash the blood away, wiped the knife and returned it to its sheath.

Peretz had a sure hand. He never needed to aim twice at any fowl or porcupine or wild pig, and never needed to strike more than once with his knife to separate a foot from a leg or a neck from a head whenever he prepared a bird for the pot.

Everyone enjoyed watching the slaughtering. The game warden set up a paraffin stove with a pot of water on it and Peretz turned to the door to bring in the slaughtered bird, when, to everyone's amazement, there was the rooster standing on the windowsill, eyes as bright as daggers, its comb erect as a coronet, and at that very moment it let out a clear call, an angry, powerful, regal "Ku-ku-ri-ku." There was a single drop of coagulated blood on its neck, like an ornamental drop of amber.

All of us started back in horror, Peretz most of all. That day he did not eat the meat of the marsh birds with gusto, in his usual manner—he ate like one whose throat was held in a vise. After a few days Naphtali discovered that Peretz was sick. "It's nothing," Peretz said to him when he visited, and tried to laugh. "My neck hurts a bit, that's all."

To cut it short, Peretz died. The hospital said it was cancer. According to common sense he died of cancer. But, as I said, common sense doesn't always make sense. "By the way," Naphtali concluded his story, "the rooster is still alive and has fathered a lot of chicks for his master since that day."

Batia pulled her hand away from Naphtali's and quickly left the roof and the house, Naphtali laughed into his liver and lit his pipe. Then he half closed his eyes and said slowly, "At last we're alone, Lysanda." "Are you sure?" she asked. Lysanda stood leaning against the wall, her eyes half closed. "What do you mean, am I sure?" he demanded angrily, "Batia's gone, isn't she?" "Is she gone?" asked Lysanda. "Of course she's gone, and good riddance." Lysanda moved her thighs gracefully and opened her eyes the tiniest crack and whispered artlessly—just as was necessary—"And you didn't give her the key?"

"What key?"

"The spare key, the one you keep hidden in the box."

I rubbed my forehead with my hand and remembered. Yes, I had given her the key and forgotten. She wanted to sit on the roof in the evenings when I was away at the newspaper. She won't disturb me, she said. She respects my work, she said. That's all she's asked me for.

And now Batia has a key to my roof.

VI

I woke up in a cabin. I knew it was a cabin right away because I had to grab hold of the bed above me to be able to stand up steadily and get dressed. Above the bed above me was another bed and above it another bed and above that one yet another bed, and so on; the beds were arranged tier upon tier upward and I couldn't see the highest one. My brother said something in a soft, fatherly tone, and I knew I had to hurry. Something great was in store for me.

I started walking quickly, and I suddenly realized that I was wearing nothing but my underpants. But I had gotten dressed in the cabin! I hurried back to the same place but found no cabin, nor any other structure. Nor did I remember what the place looked like and I wondered at this, and also at the fact that my brother, who should have been by my side, was not by my side.

I knew they were waiting for me and I didn't know where to go. I heard a voice and turned around and saw before me a huge marsh full of puddles. I stood up on my toes so as not to dirty my new shoes. I could see myself from the side and laughed at myself mockingly: he worries about his shoes but doesn't worry about drowning. A man called something to me from across the marsh, but I couldn't hear his voice. He was big and strong and I was certain I knew him, and a weakness descended over my head and my feet. I knew the man had a strong voice and I was afraid to hear it. He gestured with his hands. When I passed by him he didn't notice me, just kept waving his long, rake-like arms.

I increased my pace, dragging heavy clods of earth in my shoes. People passed to the right and to the left and paid no attention to me. I didn't see their faces, but they were wearing white shirts and spotless white trousers, and they walked with a confident step. I felt they were not my friends.

I began to doubt if this great thing had anything to do with me at all, and I couldn't understand what I was doing here. The big man appeared again in front of me and it was impossible now to see his face, for he was entirely black with mud, and he waved his long arms around in circles, one after the other, like the sails of a windmill.

I was very cold and I shrank up. I brought my shoulders down to my thighs and my back into my stomach and pitied the man as if he were me. When I awoke I was still stuck together, shoulders to thighs and back to stomach, and with all my strength I pressed myself back into the dream.

I was frightened.

VII

One night I got home from work after midnight to find the light on in my room. In the light was Batia, at work fixing up the house. My flat is a small one, and its furnishings are few. In the kitchenette are a paraffin stove and a few utensils. In the main room are a low Arab tea table, a straw armchair, two stools, some bookshelves, two or three pictures, and the bed. And at the foot of the bed a white bearskin. The room has an alcove in which stand my work table and a chair. Batia had done everything she could with this space to give it form, a form that I could not grasp. The furniture surrendered to the touch of her hands. I felt that I could go.

But the exit was guarded by Lysanda. On her face was one of her most beautiful smiles. This smile would pull her thin lips and straight teeth up toward the bulge of her cheekbones, leaving, in the space between her teeth, a darkness warmer than all love. Lysanda. She wasn't jealous. In her, everything was covered up and wide open at the same time. I knew that if I raised my hand to hit her, it wouldn't connect. This filled me with joy.

I sat down and sucked on my pipe. Lysanda loved my pipe. At times she would weave around in its smoke. I don't know why I suddenly asked about the aristocratic-looking man who had come to ask if this was where I lived and if I was me, had looked at a stuffed bird and then left—perhaps because I saw a squashed cigarette butt in the square ashtray. Who had smoked that cigarette before I got home? It couldn't have been Batia. None of her lipstick was on it. Batia answered hurriedly, "Why do you ask?" "I just want to know." Batia said, "He just came by. Just like that. 'To see,' he said." I said, "And he didn't ask if Naphtali Noi lives here?" She answered as if in on some kind of joke, "Didn't ask at all. Interesting, isn't it? He didn't ask at all." She pursed her lips mischievously, and her knee shook. I drew in some smoke and said, "But he already knows I live here and that I'm certainly me. He just came to have a peek in." "Yes, yes, he came to have a peek and left straight away," she said. "He came to peek in? Pity I wasn't here."

"Buki said you've got a nice flat," she said. "Buki?" I asked. She said, "Buki. He came, had a peek, and went." Buki? I wondered. "So it was Buki," I said, and controlled my anger.

Batia poured. It was Cointreau that I had received as a holiday gift at work and hadn't opened. Yet the bottle was no longer closed, nor was it full. She must have offered some to whoever was here, what's-his-name, Buki. Buki was a smart, bright fellow, a bit of a political climber with some Bohemian affectations, and Batia was his girlfriend. His girlfriend in between times. I had nothing against Buki. The earth can bear all types of creatures on its surface without crumbling. But I couldn't drink the liqueur.

Batia said, "Smell it." I smelled it. It had the scent of citrus buds, the scent of Lysanda's hair. "Now let's drink," said Batia. "It smells good," I said, "it's a pity to drink it." "Don't say that, don't say that," said Batia, her eyes flashing nervously, her lips closing severely. Lysanda smiled at me through the windowpane. I closed my eyes and emptied the glass with one gulp, and a harp with silver strings stretched across Lysanda's face.

"Lysanda," I said.

Batia said, "Not all at once. You don't drink Cointreau all at once. You take it in slow sips to prolong the pleasure." I drank my second and third glasses in slow sips, and Batia told me that when her husband, the sailor, used to go on long voyages—and this was the first I heard that she had been married and that her husband had been a sailor who used to go on long voyages—he would send her Cointreau and flowers for her birthdays. On her twenty-second birthday her husband the sailor was off on a long voyage and he didn't send her Cointreau and flowers. She sat on a chair on her porch for hours without moving. A friend came to visit her, another sailor, Giggie, they called him, and he had a bottle of whiskey. They drank the whiskey without talking. They finished the bottle and Giggie turned it upside down, picked her up in his arms, and carried her to the bed. There he undressed her, spread a blanket over her, and went away. "You know," she began, but didn't go on, and her eyes hurt to look at me. She took my right hand between her two hands and then laid the three hands on her knee. Her knee was not too soft and not too hard. It had been a long time since a woman's knee was so close to me. I wanted to breathe in the scent of my pipe, the scent of the calmness, the scent of lonely frightened hours. But the fire in my pipe had gone out and I needed both my hands to relight it, and a film of dark and nervous sadness misted over Batia's protuberant eyes. I couldn't pull my hand out of hers.

She may have sensed my confusion. It's a wonder that she sensed my confusion through her thick skin. Gently she gave back my hand and went out onto the roof. I heard her laughter rolling there like little stones dribbling down a slope. I went out onto the roof after her, with the bottle in my hand. The roof was moon-wrapped, and rocked like a boat, and in the corner the antenna rose like a mast. With a little black bird on top of it. I drank from the bottle, but not with great pleasure. I have never been really drunk. If I was able to get so drunk I'd forget, it's almost certain I would live not on a rooftop but in a cellar.

Batia looked at the wildfowl. It nodded its head, and Batia nodded her head and laughed a broken laugh through open teeth and called to it, "Pretty pretty," and said she was laughing at the thought of the rooster and my dead friend Peretz. I understood that the story of my dead friend Peretz and the rooster amused her a lot. Passionately she kissed the edge of a feather in the stuffed fowl's tail, and made two rounds of the roof without speaking. Then she made another round and I sucked studiously on my pipe, and she came up to me and looked into my eyes. Her eyes were bloodshot like roses. The night was warm and pink and the moon infused everything and the smoke from the pipe spread slowly from side to side without the strength to rise. I leaned my nose toward Batia's eyes to see if they really had a smell and Batia pressed them to my lips. Then we stood together and watched the lights going out all over the city and listened to the periods of stillness, to the sweat sinking into the streets that curled like wounded crocodiles. Suddenly it was sad. Batia looked at the ink-blue strip of sea and said, "You know, the sky's really close up here." I didn't want to look at the sky. I was glad the moon permeated everything. I was glad the smoke of the pipe spread outward and then fell down. "Like it's resting on the roof," Batia continued, "resting on my hair," she continued, "on my shoulders." She shrugged her shoulders.

Batia's shoulders were thick and Lysanda's shoulders were delicate. Batia's neck was strong and her hair short, while Lysanda's neck was thin and fragile, and her hair was smooth and flowing. "You can just stand here and look forever," she said. "Yes, yes," I said, "the sea's salty. You can feel its saltiness on your lips." "I love to feel its saltiness on my lips," said Batia, and licked my lips. I licked her lips. Lysanda breathed a scent of citrus buds into my ears, and even my little finger rose to greet her. "Lysanda," I said. "Who?" asked Batia. "I'll fix some coffee," I said. "No, no," said Batia, and her chest was heavy on mine. We were both the same height. All I had to do was to bend down and I would feel the warmth of a living, breathing bosom on my face where I could chew on the scented sting of a childish citron till my teeth went numb.

Batia didn't scream. She patted my head sympathetically and suggested we have some coffee. The night was heavy, compressed. Like Batia's skin, I thought. She has a skin that never sheds blood, I thought.

We had some coffee and sandwiches that Batia prepared, and finished off with more Cointreau from the square bottle that was rapidly emptying. And, feeling good, what with the Cointreau and the salty cheese sandwiches and the moon pouring down into our eyes, we began to tell each other things—details of our lives, large and small. Batia told me about her house of horrors—that's what she called her home—where they were all afraid to open the door, because every time the door opened, a new disaster entered—and her interlocutor sympathized and said, "Yes, yes, that's the way of the world." And she told about a dream she once had of becoming an actress, so that she could disguise herself as someone else and so fool the next disaster and escape it, till she began to believe that she really could change her appearance at will. And Batia laughed a very lonely laugh. And why are people so . . . I don't know what, not this and not that, it's enough to really make you cry. And she said that she liked the smell of his pipe. At the same time she tied his tie for him and said that every tie she ever tied always came to nothing ("A knotted tie lasts longer," she says). "It's degrading," she said, with great seriousness.

"Yes, yes," her interlocutor nodded his head, and Batia tells him that she doesn't love by halves. She gives herself, all of herself, in love. There could be no doubt about this—her breasts swung as she spoke, as if striving to burst out, and her heart was jumping around behind them. "Believe me, Naphtali," she said to him, "believe me, I love people, I'm built that way, I'm simply built that way." A yellow moth climbed onto her chest. One of those moths that go anyplace where it's warm. Through the smoke of his pipe he could see, on the window between the room and the roof, a pink lizard doing hunting exercises with a darting tongue. "I love people," said Batia. "Yes, yes," said Naphtali, "I love animals too." "You do?" asked Batia.

He told her that he got on fine with animals. Whatever can be stuffed, he stuffs. Spiders, butterflies, ants, lizards, and cockroaches aren't very good for stuffing. And there's no need for it, either. It's nice to see how well they get along. An ant will never get eaten up by another ant, unless it's dead. Cockroaches too, as long as they're alive, can run around in complete freedom among ants, and the ants won't touch them or try to harm them, except, perhaps, for a slight pull on one feeler or another, just for fun. Or sometime they might also turn a roach over on its back, for then it would be in their power. And it's true that lizards swallow live butterflies, but they do it very gracefully.

"Cockroaches," continued Naphtali delightedly, "are very charming little creatures that appear to have many legs only because of their great sensitivity—that is, they actually have only six legs and two feelers, each one very delicate and extremely sensitive, so that the slightest motion sets them trembling and then they flutter about in all directions, as though warding off evil spirits. It's the same with the divine Buddha, who is depicted with eight arms or more. Did Buddha the man have eight arms? But we never have enough arms to keep ourselves safe. It's wonderful to see a cockroach being carted away for burial," said Naphtali. "The ants never make a mistake. Eight ants, no more and no less, bear it away, one to each leg and to each feeler. Those with the feelers lead the procession. I don't know if there's a master of ceremonies, but the corpse is carried slowly and silently, with a kind of sacred sorrow. It never drags on the ground. It is carried as if floating on air."

Batia began to shiver. "I'm cold," she said. "Actually I'm not cold, but I'm cold," she said, and grabbed his hand nervously. Then she put down his hand and picked up a glass of Cointreau and her teeth knocked against the glass.

The night glowed with a sort of hidden warmth, and Batia told him about her limbless friend—who had had both legs amputated—a good-looking and intelligent young man. She enjoyed talking to this friend. They would sit in a café, or in his room, drinking coffee and talking, talking and laughing. A pure friendship. One day she rang his doorbell and heard his voice: "The door's open." She pushed on the door. It was indeed open. In the room, on the sofa, lay her friend, naked as on the day he was born. Though not exactly as on the day he was born, since he was limbless after all. His body was red and his stumps stuck up into the air. "This is me," he said. "Now spit on me!" he cried savagely.

Batia sunk her head into her shoulders as though trying to protect herself. The moon had gathered itself up higher and farther, and a sort of coarse and frothing mouth seemed to be chewing the roof. The night was about to be torn to tatters. I was afraid to raise my head. It was good to feel Batia's broad thighs and her heavy legs kneeling on the roof.

"Yes," said Batia, and her knees wobbled from side to side, her chest exposed to me. I was on my knees and was afraid to raise my head. The night was vanishing into the distance, and the expanses that were opening up behind it made me dizzy. Or perhaps it was the liqueur.

"How could you?" I asked.

"I was afraid of him," she said. I put my head down on her stomach. "I was disgusted by him," she said.

"Her stomach is very soft, Lysanda," I said.

"His stumps were sticking up," she said.

"I'm drunk, Lysanda," I said.

"Like swollen tendons," she said, and wrapped her arms around me.

"Her skin is thick, Lysanda," I said.

"I wanted to die," said Batia, and a wave of life shook her thighs.

"How could you?" cried Naphtali and clung to the nipples of her breasts like a hungry baby.

"I wanted to kill him," she said, and clung to me too. "I wanted him to die inside me," she said. "I wanted him to feel good," she said, "I wanted him to live," she whispered, "I wanted to give birth to him anew," she breathed. "I wanted to create him anew," she dreamed and groaned.

When Naphtali came out of her she said, "When he was in me I thought that when he came out he would come out whole and healthy." She smiled. You could see her smile. The moon was fading, about to die, and the sky was open to receive the first light, like a wounded jaw opening a doctor's eye. Her hair was short and as dry as straw. Her neck was thick. And her eyes as empty and thick as her skin. No blood flowed from it. It's true, I wanted there to be blood. Living, flowing blood, like the leaves of the poppy. My fingers twitched about restlessly.

Batia raised herself and, without bothering to straighten her clothes, wound her arms around his knees. That's quite unnecessary, thought Naphtali. He had thin knees, which looked as though they were fresh from the womb, and they were shaking a little. Batia fell asleep. A light nasal snore poured out of some opening in her skin. The roof was full of it. A light laughter burst out from somewhere nearby. Perhaps it's Lysanda laughing. I'll leave this place, he thought.

Now I'm leaving this place, he thought, and lowered his tired head into Batia's lap.

VIII

Let us return to my two sweet little gazelles, Nili and Lili (and with what joy I return to them), the two tiny candles of my life, always alight and ready to receive my thick bewildered face. Yes, very bewildered these days.

I washed my flesh delightedly. Until I heard the whistling voices of my little darlings: "Come on, Yakoko. Come on, Yakoko. Come down." And I went. And how I went.

But first I put my orange shirt over my trousers, the shirt with the four pockets, two on the heart and two on my hips that were now jumping for joy, and in each of the pockets I put toffees and sweets, so that wherever my beloved ones sent their little hands they would find them. And they, my little dears, would fill my pockets with ash and cigarette butts from their father's ashtrays, and banana peel and watermelon seeds from Mrs. Schturz's kitchen garbage. And with their tiny feet jumping their voices would ring:

Yakoko my koko
Go get us some choko
Yah kee yah koko
Yah koko riko

and they would laugh till they could laugh no more. And when they could laugh no more, they would throw things at me, anything in reach, and kick me with their little feet, and finally, gasping like delighted puppies, they would jump onto my knees, each onto her own knee, Nili on the right one (she is the firstborn) and Lili on the left, and they would both call out:

"So tell us, what happened to the witch?"

"I'll tell you the story from the beginning," I said. In any case, I had forgotten the story I had told them yesterday and the one I had told the day before yesterday and the one I had told the day before that. To tell the truth, it's the same story in different variations.

"From the beginning," twittered my little darlings. The skin of their arms and thighs was thin and transparent. Looking at it, all my demons became angels, and all the witches fairies.

I tell them the story about the king who never laughs. For the king loves the girl of his dreams, who appeared to him once in his childhood, and since then he has never laughed. He never laughs, but the people of his kingdom laugh. So he makes terrible trouble for them, beats them a bit and hits them and shoots them and hangs them on trees for the wind and the crows. And my little ones shudder on my knees happily and impatiently. And the miserable, laughing people of the kingdom bring before their king who never laughs a young orphaned shepherd girl (one of those young orphaned shepherd girls who were meant to marry princes) who says she saw, in the cave in the woods, a beautiful maiden combing her long hair in front of a mirror lit by two candles. And the king who never laughs immediately commands that the beautiful maiden be brought from the woods—and all the time I'm thinking where and how to fit the witch into the picture, for a story without a witch is simply not a story for my two little angels; at times their eyes light up as if they themselves were two little witch-girls. And here I sin a mighty sin against poetics and change the plot midstream: the king's men accompany the little shepherd girl, but it is not a beautiful maiden they find in the cave in the woods—it's a witch. They bring her before the king. And the witch says to the king (as she caresses the owls on her arm with long veiny fingers), "I shall fulfill your wish, O King, and I want neither silver nor gold, for what would a witch do with silver and gold. But do this: set aside a room for me in your palace, with a mirror and a candle and nothing else in it, and at one minute after midnight come down to the room, and you shall find the maiden your heart desires. Only swear to me that you will not touch her, not even with your little finger."

The king swears, and when the hour comes and the beautiful maiden is standing before the king, all bathed in light—the beauty of his dreams—the king forgets the oath he has sworn, and approaches her and touches her with his hand. That, really, is how I meant to tell it to my eager little listeners. But instead of this Naphtali Noi said to them, "As soon as the king who never laughs saw her, he began to laugh. And he laughed and laughed, laughed so much until—" I felt a tightening in my throat and began to cough and splutter.

"Till they got married," continued Nili and Lili. Little demons.

"No," I said. "No. The king just touched her and right away the beautiful maiden turned into a witch."

"The witch from the woods?" asked my darlings and squirmed on my knees in excitement.

"Yes," I said.

"With no teeth in her old mouth and lots and lots of wrinkles?" Suddenly their position on my knees became uncomfortable to them. They looked at me out of their big eyes, slowly slid down from my knees and then looked at each other with great seriousness. Many, many sights passed through their sad eyes. Then, as though everything had become clear to them, their eyes lit up again and in a sudden outburst Nili cried:

"A witch like Aunt Kapusta."

"Yes, like Aunty Kapusta," repeated Lili.

"Who's Aunt Kapusta?" I asked.

"Come on, Yakoko, come on, Yakoko," they shouted and pulled me by my two hands and dragged me out onto the staircase, and led me down one flight and looked into the keyhole of a door which bore a small copper plate with the inscription RACHEL KAPUSTA.

I looked through the keyhole and saw an old woman lying on a bed, covered up to her neck with a clean sheet; one hand which poked out of the sheet was hanging down and the other was pressing a picture to her heart with thin contorted fingers that looked very long in their thinness, and her face was yellow and her mouth open and empty of teeth. Her lips, her nostrils, did not move, and her hand was still over her heart. There was no doubt—the woman was dead. I was confused. Dead people always confuse me. They never listen. The little girls got frightened suddenly and held each other tightly. Maybe they saw something on my face. I told them to call their mother, to show this to their mother. I tried to imagine Mrs. Schturz's face, so swollen with life and energy, when she looked through the keyhole.

I wanted to put my hand into my pocket. But my pocket was stuck shut with chewing gum. The naughty creatures! What a fluttering of life there was in that chewing gum.

IX

Batia has a big chin. Big and powerful. Maybe the Creator's hand slipped, for somehow this firm chin doesn't fit in with Batia's abundant—and sometimes painful—femininity. I sometimes feel that her chin is descending on me, reaching for me from every part of Batia's body. It is what the French call *de trop*. Not just the chin— she is all *de trop*. All of her. My whole Batia. A bath of mercury. A bed of roses. A tomb of sweetness. A man walks along and smells flowers, then walks along wallowing in mud and smells flowers, then walks along wallowing in mud and no longer smells flowers, then walks along and is just—wallowing in mud. But, during those first days, between Naphtali and Batia there was only the smell of flowers.

Perhaps I wouldn't have sunk myself into her so deeply, up to my very fingertips, if, on leaving the joy-nest of my little doves Nili and Lili, I hadn't looked through that keyhole and seen Mrs. Kapusta lying there so dead. That had been death in all its ugliness. There was nothing alive around her. Not even a fly resting on her open mouth. She had lain there for days and nobody knew. Then you leave the house and you're afraid to shut the door behind you; you hear footsteps at night, in the silent street, and you're afraid to turn your head around; you see the wind descending on your roof—Oh, my sweet little tomb! Orgy of forgetfulness! My honey pit! Slow bitter dribble of time!—Batia's breasts drip it into my flesh. And to what shall I compare her smell? To the bittersweet smell of the citron. The citron is a holy fruit. It is kept for the sacred rites in a glass case itself resembling a breast. It rests in cotton wool, and babies' fingers are always reaching for it, and small mouths are always drawn to its tip.

Batia spread out uncaring as the earth, her big eyes open. If two pits were to yawn open in the earth, they would look like her two eyes at such moments. She lay as if unaware of her two treasures, the golden juice of her nipples, the wondrous white substance (her breasts had never seen the sun or the air and were as white and submissive as cotton wool). And his lips burned like desert sands. And then, in all its apathy, the wonderful earth began to quake and open wide its mercy, and his teeth tightened like the teeth of a hyena on a chicken's neck.

And a little eye looked on from the side, laughing.

X

This little eye of Naphtali's, that peeps out at the moments of greatest excitement to laugh its nasty, mocking laugh—that little eye was very busy these days. But the eye was one thing, and Naphtali another. And the proof: Naphtali Noi's face and behavior in those days.

His face was a sort of good-heartedness. Lukewarm, lackluster, a kind of comfortable dullness. The light that used to hide deep in his eyes and give them the appearance of being turned inside out moved to the corners now, and his eyes grew clear. At the newspaper they began addressing him by his first name, and when in absentmindedness he overlooked some spelling errors, the typesetters were pleased (fewer corrections) and the editors became angry and made remarks about this to him without polite preliminaries like, "Mr. Noi," "We have noticed," and, "Perhaps you could—" which they had had to employ previously. Things went so far that one day the office boy came up to him, slapped him on the back, and said, "It's hot today." And Naphtali replied, "Yes, it is." For it really was hot.

In those days his thoughts began drifting toward a new subject to write about an article, to which he mentally gave the title, "Erotic Elements in (Primitive) Israelite Symbols and Myths," and what he was really getting at was *Sukkot*, the feast of Tabernacles, but not the entire Feast of Tabernacles, just the Hosannah prayer of the Feast of Tabernacles, and not the entire Hosannah prayer, the waving of the palm branch and the citron in the Hosannah prayer—that holy union of the erect palm branch and the oval citron. He had already written the title at the head of a blank page, and at one point he even drew a citron under it with its nipple a point. But for some reason he had turned the page over. Those were lazy days, spent in a comfortable stupor.

At times, in the sweltering hours of the afternoon, after Batia's return from work and after a hasty meal, as they lay naked in their acidic sweat, Batia would beg him to read her what he had written in the morning. Batia could not know, of course, that Naphtali had not written a thing in the morning—not this morning, nor any of the previous mornings, since the day they had become intimate. She was certain that just as she had improved his life as a whole, she had given momentum to Naphtali Noi's creative spirit; and it is probable that had she known the truth, she would have become very distressed, like a person making an unappreciated sacrifice. Naphtali was very cautious about this, and he would read her extracts from his various writings—things he had not yet published or that he had not yet gotten ready for the press. And when he reached a point in his article that seemed a little unfinished, unclear, obscure, she would raise the upper part of her body, so that her two citrons, swollen with life, would part from her trunk, and she would look at him, her confused treasure, who had so much wisdom, though of a strange kind, and her big eyes would narrow a little, as though looking at him straight from the very wellspring of pity and grace. And her confused treasure, who all this time was still reading, hearing nothing but the sound of his monotonous voice, could already sense his dream dispersing, and all his body strained and stiffened and swayed toward her in thanks. Later she would pick up the crumpled and moist pages that still smelled of sweat, straightening them out carefully and scolding him: "Why don't you look after them? Look after them. These pages are very important."

"Ve-ry im-por-tant"—these two words twisted slowly and incomprehensibly in his consciousness, and he understood that he had to get up—this was what Batia wanted—and taste the apple tart she had bought on the way home, and drink some sweetened lemon juice from the refrigerator. Afternoon "tea" spiced with light conversation. Hers, about her circle of acquaintances, and his about the world at large. Batia greatly admired his words, and kept asking for more of them, while her foot tapped the floor with a real thirst for knowledge; then all the alternately smooth and mossy, shady glades of her body that appeared through her bathrobe were as still as a sunny landscape at noon. At times like this Naphtali would make an effort to swallow all his yawns and disinterest, so as not to anger Batia.

"You know what time it is?" she asked suddenly, and her face widened out in a smile, to show him how quickly the hours had passed without being noticed. Naphtali knew what time it was from the calls of Nili and Lili down in Mrs. Schturz's apartment: "Come on Yakoko / Why don't you come Yakoko / Bad boy Yakoko—" If he goes down to them he will tell them that the sad king married the beautiful maiden. The time was a superfluous question. He had put his wristwatch down on the little tea table (which Batia had brought) and forgotten it was there.

Each morning they would rise with the birds that filled the roof with their twittering. ("Birds make love in the morning," said Batia.) Then they would have breakfast. Batia would wish him a productive day's work, and go off to work herself. After her heavy footfalls had died upon the staircase, he would go back to bed and drowse. In any case he was in no mood for doing anything. Two owls lay on their backs with open bellies, ready for stuffing. Their heads were off and lay beside them. Before meeting Batia he had wanted to liberate their neckless heads from their bodies and to have them "bobble" in the air upon spiral necks; now he looked at them in confusion. He passed the wildfowl and didn't look at it—he only dusted its tail a little. He watered the flowers and plants without thinking. He didn't test the soil with his finger to see if it was dry or not, if he had to add a little water or a lot, if it was necessary to break up the dry crust of topsoil. And of course he pruned nothing, nor did he try to improve creation by giving new form to those colorful life forms. Mornings like this he would chew on his little pipe, the bowl of which looked like the head of a bull whose horns, he thought, in the fog of his mind and the glare of the sun, resembled two proud moustache ends rising up from under his nose.

He withdrew inside, closed the shutters, and in the ensuing dimness came across Batia in every corner—in the hairpins she had scattered everywhere—on the bookshelves, the tea table, the floor, the bed and the bathroom—in the transparent black petticoat that lay bundled up like a kitten on the straw stool, in the sweet and acid smell that mingled with the smoke of his pipe and filled the room with titillating dreams.

He would sit for long hours at his worktable, pipe in mouth, pen in hand, with a blank sheet of paper before him. He would sit like a still and silent statue, a memorial of a some ancient life. At other times he would slip along with the bony fingers of light through the slits in the shutter that looked like the slots of a mailbox. Then he would jump up, fall full-length on the couch and wrap his head—oh the shame of it—in Batia's petticoat.

Every evening he would come home and climb up the stairs and play a guessing game with himself. He tried to guess if Batia was at home. Of course he knew that Batia was at home, but the game filled him with a pleasant tension, and when he heard the heavy breathing, or at times the snoring, of his Batia, the tension relaxed, and, also breathing heavily from climbing the stairs and from something else as well, he would call, "I was afraid you wouldn't come." Batia would wake up and without opening her eyes would tell him what he would find in the refrigerator ("Egg salad and a leg of chicken / Stuffed peppers / Kidneys with potatoes but heat it up a little").

At times when he got home he would be bothered by a strange smell, the smell of cigarette smoke. Of course Batia also smoked, but this was not her smoke, this was not her smell. Then he would stop short for a moment in the doorway, like someone trying to get to his legs to march into the line of fire, and then he would go in, without asking any questions, but his appetite would diminish to a startling degree. And the little eye would look on from the side, a little larger and more amused than usual.

XI

Batia told me about a nightmare she often had about a man and a candle. The man is her father, and the candle—a lit candle in his hand. The dream pursues her, she said. An innocent pigeon put its foot down on a flowerpot on the roof. The flowerpot, which had not been standing very firmly, swayed, the pigeon flew off, the flowerpot fell and landed on an empty pail, and the empty pail, at this late hour after midnight, gave out a sound like the clashing of cymbals. Batia's body shuddered, her breath stopped, and all her fingers dug into my shoulders as though she was holding on for dear life. She was thoroughly panic-stricken. She shook a little and kept opening her mouth as though trying to say something, but didn't make a sound. I switched on the light. After she had calmed down and caught her breath, she told me her dream.

In her dream she is sleeping in a small room, perhaps in a tent. (Her mother had told her that when Batia was a little girl they had been very poor and had slept in a tent. Her father, so Batia's mother told Batia and Batia told me, had left the house and had never been heard of again.) Suddenly she senses that her father is standing on her bed and looking at her. And warmth fills her, together with a touch of fear. She says, "Hello, Papa, have you come back?" And he says, "Yes, my daughter, I have come to take you." And then she feels that her mother isn't in the room and she says, "But turn on the light, Papa, I can't see a thing." And then she's already certain that her mother is gone, and her father lights a candle and raises it slowly, and she wonders at the fact that as he raises the candle she cannot see his hand. But she can clearly see what he's wearing—a kind of hairy, brownish Arab robe. And when he raises the candle up to his face she recognizes his pipe (Batia's mother had told her that her father smoked a pipe and sat around all day thinking and doing nothing), and his pipe is fixed between two rows of bared teeth, and in the place of his eyes are two black holes and his face is the face of a skull. And she is terribly frightened, because she thinks that Papa is sick and she wants to call out, "Mama," but she can't shout. Here she always woke up and had to try out her throat to see if she still had a voice.

Not the most pleasant dream, but even though it was generally accompanied by the blind fear that she would no longer be able to talk or to sing (Batia liked to sing sentimental ballads), it didn't really seem that she was struggling with great dread. Her vitality, which was *de trop*, like everything else about her, kept her safe on all sides, and horror stories were, to tell the truth, just a harmless amusement for us both. The story of her love for the young man with the stumps was no less horrible than the dream, and perhaps packed more of a punch; but it was, at any rate, more complete, more aesthetic, to Naphtali's anti-naturalistic taste. I would perhaps have preferred it had her father lived in Jerusalem, say, and had met her and told her that on this or that night he too had dreamed, and in his dream he was standing on Batia's bed and looking down at her. Or perhaps—and this is particularly appealing to me—if she had dreamed that her father turns to her mother and says, "Chana, light the candles," and her mother lights the candles and passes her hands over them in blessing, and only then, when she moves her hands away from the candles, is the skull revealed.

That night I slipped out of bed very cautiously, so that Batia wouldn't notice, and went to the kitchen window that looks out onto the wall of the house next door. The house was plunged in the darkness left by a high and squeezed-dry moon. Shadows lengthened—a yellowish-gray wall and square black windows. One of them was the window through which I always used to see the round table with its white tablecloth and burning candles. The table was where it always stood and the cloth wasn't exactly white, but I could imagine it was white, and the two candles weren't exactly alight, but I could imagine they were alight—a very thin light, coming from them like a reflection off of copper. Suddenly I was afraid that they might actually be out and that I was only imagining they were alight. How well I knew this cursed feeling—fear—this feeling I had known before I met Batia.

The next day I waited patiently beside the drainpipe in the bathroom, and as soon as I heard first the yawns and then the other sounds of Mr. Schturz leaving the house, I put my pipe down, filled my pockets with sweets, and rushed down to the Schturz apartment with all the speed that my characteristic restraint would allow my feet. I met my two little ones like two tugs at my heart, my little forgotten darlings, so wonderful, so gazelle-like. Even the angry and resentful gaze of Mrs. Schturz (That weird babysitter from the roof! She entrusts her children to him, and he, ungrateful creature, stays away for days, and ruins the best hours of her day!) made no impression on him.

But after he had picked himself up from the floor of sweet tortures, on which the little ones had rolled him hither and thither with graceful kicks—a few kicks for him and a few for the doll with the golden plait—he went up to their large window and looked out.

The window opposite, in the house next door, was shut. The shutter wasn't closed—perhaps it was broken. The window frame was very old, with nail marks in its corners, the paint was peeled off in various layers, like a window that had been painted many times until it had finally been left alone, and through the dusty pane he saw a round table. That was all. There was nothing else there, no candlesticks and no candles, and of course—no light. It looked like a room in which no one had lived for a very long time. On the other hand, on the wall of Mrs. Schturz's bedroom, opposite the window of the closed house, and at the same height, hangs a painting of lighted candlesticks. I don't know how Mrs. Schturz feels about this innocent painting, but it moves my heart to see it. The candlesticks, of silver, are exquisite, and the candles are white as cotton wool and the two flames are yellow, oleaginous and radiant. It seems that the artist didn't skimp on the paint here, and the gray around the flames only makes their light stand out, and it's the tiny bed lamp that stays on all night next to the picture that casts their reflection onto the old window of the deserted room opposite. Actually I could have discovered all this a long time ago. If I had wanted to.

So Batia had been right, that first night when I showed her the lighted candles. She had laughed and said there was nothing there. Hadn't she seen the reflection of these good, humble, real candles there in the window? She almost certainly must have seen them and understood; her laugh had been nervous—perhaps she had remembered her dream—and I didn't notice it at the time. In any case I was angry with her that she hadn't seen what I had seen. That it should turn out like this—that it was I who saw what *she* had seen!

I hurried down to the entrance of the house and moved my mailbox. I used long steel nails. Next to it hung a list of the tenants of the house, floor by floor. On the second floor a straight line had been drawn, perhaps with the aid of a ruler, across the name of Mrs. Kapusta. She had certainly been buried by now. I walked to and fro on the roof, ferreting around among my materials and examining my owls, my fingers like tensed strings. I exchanged one pipe for another—the pipes that sat so cozily in their nests, each one awaiting its turn, had a strange effect on my palate now, and the roof seemed to let go its stubborn squareness, and to burst and leak out from its corners. I decided to put things in order a bit.

First of all I picked up Batia's black petticoat, which was resting like a slovenly old hen on the stool, folded it nicely and put it away in the cupboard.

XII

"Who knows the nature of fear? A man walks along like any other man, in a street like any other street, with its vehicles and people and noise, and then he sees a little gray pebble and he kicks it; the little gray pebble is turned over on its back—and it's a beetle. Lying on its back, little and gray, waving its little legs in the air.

"I deliberately didn't begin with examples that speak for themselves, like the sight of lightning, the sound of a stifled cry at night, an empty sleeve hanging on a washing line, a shadow passing across your face (perhaps your own), the sound of footsteps in an empty street (perhaps your own), and so on and so on. I deliberately did not bring up any of these and brought up an imaginary pebble. Just to show that fear resides in the dust of the earth.

"Leah once said to me that a child closes itself in a square and is afraid to come out of it. He screams when the square is forced open. At times without a sound, for he is frightened. Toys in squares, cubes, hopscotch on the pavement, the squareness of rooms, etc. I said to her, 'I think that adults are the same—a man grows, and the square grows with him.' "

Why did I write this? Anyhow, the roof I live on is square-shaped.

XIII

I read somewhere that a woman can sniff you out just as well in a heap of garbage or in a pile of peacock feathers. Tonight my Batia sat up looking at me until my eyelids started hurting. I was forced to open them. "You weren't sleeping," she said.

"I was sleeping," I protested. I was a little angry at her because I was ashamed of having pretended to be asleep. Apart from that, a little while ago I had seen Lysanda—she hadn't come to me for weeks and I hadn't even felt her absence—she seemed a bit ashamed and I didn't know if it was because of me or herself. She had been dressed like a page boy. "I was sleeping," I said.

"Maybe," said Batia and smiled affectionately, "but your eyes tell me a different story." "How can you see that in my eyes?" "And I see something else too." "What?" "Fear." "Fear?" "And hate." "Hate?" "Hate's better than apathy." I relaxed and embraced her. I'm not sure, but maybe I really did want to embrace her. Anyhow, that way she couldn't look into my eyes anymore.

"You can't sleep, my poor darling," she said.

"Yes."

"You want to kill me," she said all of a sudden. "Why don't you take a pill or something," she continued in the same even tone. She bent the upper part of her body over my face, and it looked heavy and brown in the dim light, like a hibernating tree, and she wiggled it from side to side, and the tips of her nipples tickled my eyes, my nose and my lips. Lysanda in her page-boy clothes had no breasts at all.

"Please don't," I said.

"Maybe you're cold, you'd better get under the blanket so you'll feel warmer, you'd better cover yourself up, you'll feel warmer and then you'll be able to sleep"—and she continued rocking her torso over me to a singsong rhythm like: "In the surge of the seas in the blaze of the days in the burn of the brine with the burden so blind on the waters—"

"Lysanda," I whispered with closed eyes. The rest you know.

XIV

I looked into the bathroom mirror. An old mirror, slightly cracked. The face that looked out at me was pleasant and cheerful, almost jovial. As though it enjoyed looking at me. Like the face of a cook delightedly watching you gobble up a dish he's prepared for you, imperceptibly imitating the blinking of your lips and the leaps of your Adam's apple and the tension of your jaw and temples and the raising of your eyebrows and the fluttering of your nostrils. A round, satiated face—one could almost say good-looking. Curly hair close to the head like a Greek wrestler's. An intelligent forehead, a straight nose, big bright eyes, though a little too bright. I don't like a satiated face, and when I pass one in the street I look away.

But here, in the mirror, it even appealed to me a bit. I put my pipe in my mouth and took it out, because it pleased me to see how this face, as it spread its lips around the pipe, took on gravity without losing any of its spiritual beauty. You could sit down to a pleasant chat with someone like that, a chat garnished with pleasant platitudes, and you wouldn't expect to hear any startling innovations—or even any slightly depressing ones—such as those lavished upon the few, the very few, who happen to find themselves in Naphtali Noi's presence.

But then I look into the mirror again and see that in the corners of his eyes a little man is drowning in a vast sea. (Ha, fear!) The face is transfigured. A short sharp crease from the nose to the corners of the mouth. The upper lip pulling inward, as if bitten from inside. The right eyebrow raised as if surprised, and two purplish crescents of cheek, in which the eyes are fixed, trembling with a slight twitch, so slight it's barely noticeable.

XV

One morning Batia woke up sick. That same morning I got up with a wondrous sweetness flowing through my bones—something that rarely happens to me. A forgotten dream permeated my flesh and I didn't know what it could be. I only remembered that in the middle of the night I had gotten up, and it was dark. I had tried the light switch in the doorway to the bathroom but it hadn't worked. I had gone out onto the roof, taken a candle out of my toolbox and lit it. There was no light in any of the windows on the street, and the street lamps were out. Must be a power failure, I said to myself. A slice of moon was alight above. I raised the candle toward the moon that now looked like the apple that Mother Eve had taken a bite of.

The flame flickered. I was sure Lysanda was breathing on it with her scented breath. There is something wonderful about candlelight, something ritual, magical. I remembered that in my childhood I saw an Indian fakir concentrating his gaze on the flame of a candle till he fell down open-eyed in a holy trance. And in fact they buried him in that position and when they took him back out of the ground he got up and shook himself as if coming out of a dream.

That was at the circus. I could understand that man. My Lysanda—a black velvet sash around her waist, two tiny golden crescents dangling from the nipples of her pale, transparent cup-like breasts—was standing behind me. Unfortunately I was unable to develop this pleasant scene further because I was in a hurry to see to my other needs. When I came back from there, I stopped by Batia's bed and covered the flame with my free hand.

Two or three fine jets of light fell on the sleeper's face. One of them grazed her eyelids. Batia's breathing stopped for a moment, and then she burst into short, panic-stricken yells. I put out the candle.

In the morning Batia's face looked pretty bad: a blue line under her eyes, cheeks burning, and the pupils of her large eyes were darting around nervously.

The sight of her face frightened me not a little and I asked her how she felt.

"I don't know what's wrong with me," she said. She asked me to see if there was anything in her throat. I saw nothing except for the uvula that was jumping up and down as if it didn't feel at home in there. I told her that I couldn't see anything special. She told me that on waking up she had felt pains in her throat, as if there was lead in her windpipe. She drank some coffee and felt a little better. "My head," she said, "phew! I can't remember when I had a headache as bad as this." I caressed her head and said, "It'll pass, Batia, it'll pass." "'Course it'll pass," said Batia.

Her amazing optimism touched me. "We can't let this wonderful head hurt," I said and caressed her head again.

She placed her head against my chest and said in a different voice, "Something happened." "What?" I asked. "Something," she said. "Something terrible?" I asked. "Something terrible," she said, "I had the dream with the candle." "With the candle?" I asked. "With the candle," she said, "and I was sinking, sinking—" And Batia grasped me tight with both her arms.

I removed her arms from me quickly and said, "We can't just let you be sick. I'll call the doctor." True, Batia and I are not legally married. But it's a fact that in every way we live like a married couple. She lives in my home—I mean our home. We share our meals, our incomes, our sheets, and almost every afternoon we exchange opinions on all sorts of things. And if I don't look after her when she's in trouble, who will? I may have been a bit rough the way I tore myself out of her arms, but I'm sure Batia will understand that only my concern for her made me get up so quickly from the bed—on which she'll be able to rest and relax now, all by herself—and made me rush, without waiting for breakfast, to the doctor's.

XVI

The first crack in the wall is a bad sign; not only don't you expect it to go away, you fear its expansion, you dread another crack, and another, and so on—until the city comes to evacuate the ruins.

At first sight there seems to be no connection to the progress of Batia's illness. True, in the first days her situation was serious. The doctor ordered complete rest and prescribed some medications, and I trudged from drugstore to drugstore. Her little plans, her pretty hopes, to get up, to go out, to get some fresh air, to do this or that, the plans that Batia wove under the influence of her medicine—fell to pieces in the long hours of pain that came more and more often as her drugs wore off.

But Batia hoped. Her chin may have sunk a little, but she hoped. This optimism was doubtlessly her strong point. It seemed that she had adapted herself to the miserable rhythm of her sickness: medicine brought on hours of relief, hours of relief brought on hopes and plans, hopes and plans brought on long hours of suffering, and then—the redeeming angel, Naphtali Noi, appeared, with a new medication in hand. And at times—yes—with a little present as well, to sweeten her suffering a bit.

What didn't I bring her during those days, during that first week of her sickness: a plaster monkey, a clay jug, a clown carved out of wood, and once I even brought her a silver-plated copper bracelet, which fit her wrist and completely and amazingly covered an ugly scar dating back to her childhood games, when, for lack of decent toys at home, she had mostly played in the junk and refuse outside their house. I do not deny the science of medicine, but this bracelet conquered Batia's pains no less, and perhaps more, than the drugs. And, I may add—also gave some pleasure to Naphtali, who for a long time had grown weary of looking at that scar, which reminded him of a rough seam in one of his mounted animals.

Gradually there was a slight improvement in her health. The nightmare left her, and although her fear of it disturbed her rest, particularly at night, her voice began to get clearer. At first her voice sounded like a rusty shutter wrenched out of place. Then her windpipe opened up completely and let it out at last. She touched up her hair and face a little and went out for a walk—and I gladly encouraged her in this.

As is usual in cases like these, the doctor only bothered to look in after she'd began to recover. He advised Batia to get plenty of fresh air and warned her against getting excited. As he said this, the doctor was looking at me. And I did keep her from getting excited, to the best of my ability. To make it clear to her that I intended to carry out the doctor's instructions, I got myself a folding bed. Sometimes I even had to use little tricks: an urgent meeting that I would invent when Batia wanted to shower me with her everlasting love; or, "Just a moment, I left my pipe burning on the table, it might start a fire," in response to the battle cry of her flaming body. "Health above all!" I would say to Batia.

At times Batia would come back from her walk with a light and excited flush on her pale face and a glow in her eyes, and she would look at me and leer shamelessly. I will not deny that the thought that I had finally taken her out of the arms of that politician-son-of-a-shopkeeper, what's his name, Buki, delighted me now and then. But on second thought I found that it was not this which really filled my heart with joy, but something more exalted, something that was rooted in the fact of Batia's being both mine and someone else's, or Batia's being only mine and afterward only someone else's, and after that some other person's again, and so on, and after all that—Batia returning to my roof to shudder at the sight of the stuffed wildfowl with one eye looking upward and the other down. Of course Naphtali always retreated to his second thought, in which everything became a riddle, every riddle a challenge, and every challenge a tiny dread. And at times a great one.

The box of materials and tools was never closed now. The roof had become a studio. I pulled apart a little mountain swallow (that my former teacher Sternik had sent me in a moment of conscience) that looked like a trident, and stuck four additional wings on it; I didn't know where to put its little head. I spread a kind of canopy, like a bat's wing, over the ribs of a pigeon and hid its head among its feathers; I didn't know what to do with its legs. I gathered feathers and, carefully selecting the shapes and the colors, put them together in the round tail of a fan. It was a wonderful combination of shapes and colors. I stuck it up on the antenna post at the corner of the roof. Perhaps the wind would blow through it. But I wasn't satisfied. I sat for hours, enclosed within myself, still, unmoving, praying voicelessly, till I got up and extracted a fiery orchid made of strips of colored plastic and threads of steel wire out of the swollen belly of an owl. I put it up as a sentry, to keep away the noises of the street, the voices of the earth. I liked watching its flaming wings flaring and fluttering in all directions. But the sight of its plastic skin and iron depressed me. The last straw.

In those days Naphtali Noi devised many ruses in order to call forth all his creative powers. He refrained from eating and drinking during working hours. From time to time he washed his hands, soaked his forehead, trimmed the nails of his fingers and toes. In his mouth he held an unlit pipe of coarse oakwood, neither painted nor varnished, with its bowl pointing downward. He removed all Batia's things from inside (hid them in the cupboard) and before he had fathomed why he was doing it he moved his work inside off of the roof, and closed the doors and the shutters. The days were hot, and he sweated a lot without the windows open, and the more he sweated the more he bathed his skin in cold water and scrubbed his body with clean towels, till the stench of cleanliness refreshed his spirits. After all this, particularly after finishing some new piece of work, he would find himself standing from time to time with arms drooping beside his body, like unwanted limbs, his head fallen on his chest, looking but not seeing, thinking but not knowing about what. No, not like this. Not like this.

In this state he would stand for hours without moving; his innards slowly flowing and pouring away—kidneys, liver, stomach, lungs, heart—and he growing shorter and smaller, with his skin fluttering and trembling and his tiny hand seeming to want a large strong hand to hold on to. But no large hand would reach out to him, and the hours of weakness would come to an end not like a sponge being, squeezed slowly dry, but all of a sudden, like the slamming of a door, and Naphtali Noi would resume his work where he had left off, fending off his desolate hours as one fends off a grain of dust with a flick of the eyelid; yet the grains of dust gather and settle on your shoulders, layer upon layer, and the more the eyes of your spirit rise, the more your shoulders lower and slump.

XVII

I had expected better treatment from the dream purveyor. After all, I've been a good client of his. Thousands, yes, I say this without exaggeration, I have dreamed thousands of dreams at the expense of hours of sleep, and so—naturally enough—of repose. There are those who ask dreams questions and dreams answer them, they say. Then there are those who the dreams question, and so they answer or try to answer. My dreams—what are they?—floating shadows, an invisible tumult, vanishing smoke that leaves a smoldering in the eyes, a bitter and sometimes icy smoldering on waking. Wisps like tails, slipping through my grasping hands. Burlesques.

For what can be the meaning of the dream I had about Mrs. Kapusta being carried to her grave, and suddenly it's not she lying in the coffin but Batia! And Batia raises her head and smiles at me and I calm down the angry pallbearers and assure them that I stuffed her with first-grade seaweed. Silly. And it was such a long dream. Then I woke up. And that's all I remember.

Or this wretched memory from another dream. Shouts: "Lysanda!" And the shouts are coming from a number of directions at once. But whichever way I turn my head—she's not there. And Mr. Schturz's eyes, cold and furious, staring at me incessantly. And I know they're dangerous. Or: I am looking at a suitcase, a crowd and me. All of us are looking at it, but somehow the others are looking at me as well.

The suitcase is my mailbox—that's obvious to me from the start. But I feel it is also more than that. Not a mailbox but a trap, a mine, a snare. And the others wait. That's all I remember of that dream. By the way, a special sort of letter, precise in style and correct in all the rules of syntax, was stuck on to my mailbox a few days ago. I couldn't say exactly when. A letter of warning. I don't remember what I did with the letter. At times I feel that the boundary between dream and reality is growing more and more confused, and this makes me rejoice. Yes. Anyhow, I shall write about the letter later.

One dream I do remember. A short, humble dream that, when I awoke, rested patiently on my eyelashes. And it is still there—on my eyelashes. On the eyelashes of my being, which flutter so much these days. I stumble over feet in the dreams and the feet are in felt slippers and the slippers are soft and creased like a hippopotamus's head. And then, very frightened, I hear a man's voice. I don't remember what the man said, nor could I reach him because of the crowd. I wanted to help him find me. He passed by me and I was afraid he would pass me by. I called something to him but I don't know what it was. Perhaps he didn't hear my voice or perhaps he did hear my voice but didn't see me. I hurriedly lit a candle. I knew that by candlelight he would recognize me.

And now to that warning letter. A few days ago—as I said, I don't remember exactly when—I went down to inspect the position of my mailbox. I had grown accustomed to finding it in a different place each day and I will not deny that in this I found a certain pleasure. But now for the first time I found that the name Naphtali Noi, which I had written on the box in small but tidy letters, had been crossed out with a line that was neither straight nor tidy, as if meant to cross out more than just my name. And if this was not enough, over the whole front of the box hung a square sheet of paper, carefully printed in block letters, and it was clear that it had been copied out a number of times.

It began by stating that in spite of previous warnings (what warnings?) I had continued to put up my mailbox in a position that blocked the light switch to the staircase from the view of people entering the house. As a consequence, the letter claimed, the electrical connection had been damaged (aha—the long nails!) and now the light on the staircase was out of order, endangering everyone who entered the building, tenants and visitors alike, who now faced the risk of falling over in the dark and breaking their legs. And so they threatened me with legal action, "unless, sir, you immediately repair the electricity and leave your mailbox in the place we have designated. The Tenants." And then followed the names of all the tenants, floor by floor, from the bottom to the top. Not a name was missing.

It is unnecessary to say that first of all I put the mailbox back in its original place. But I did not touch the warning letter. As a proofreader, I was pleased with the neat and precise lettering of the petition. I appreciate a beautiful thing, even when done by people who wish me ill, who draw a line, a crooked line, across my name, across my very existence. I fled to my roof.

XVIII

I have learned something that's given me a shock. All those days that Batia walked around pale and anguished and out of breath, all the days of her sickness, when I cared for her, brought her medicine, and obeyed the doctor's orders not to touch her, to keep her from undue excitement; all those days, I say, and particularly in the evenings when I worked late—Batia would meet Buki and make love with him. I must admit, this in itself was not what shook me. Nor was it the fact that these trysts took place in my flat, my rooftop flat, and, as it seems—on my bed—the bed of my fears and dreams. The creatures of my spirit—the wondrous stuffed birds that ornament my square roof—are my witness that I did not hold a grudge against my poor, good-hearted Batia. There was something novel in the fact that my Batia—yes, mine, in spite of all—that it was she who told me about it, in great agitation, with her own lips. But, actually, that wasn't what shocked me, exactly. I should describe these things in their proper order. Evening. Heat. Sunset. Facing the sea. The moon has not risen yet, but its footsteps resound on the roof (my last moon—mysterious—cruel—). Naphtali, bare-headed, barefooted, in ragged trousers, his shirt torn at the shoulder, a pipe in his mouth, works, completely absorbed, on his stuffed birds. He burns something, breaks off his humming, takes the pipe out of his mouth, backs away from the work of his hands, approaches again, wipes his forehead with a trembling hand. His eyes suddenly glitter with a brilliant flash of cunning, of madness. But it passes. Lysanda is hidden behind the bird. Naphtali mumbles something. Lysanda answers him from inside the bird. Naphtali calls to Lysanda. The door opens. Batia.

Batia thought that I didn't see her. That's what she claims. But I definitely saw her come in. I can even describe her clothes and the look on her face. She was wearing a cocoa-colored pleated dress, long and wide (her feminine instincts led her to cover her heavy thighs with flaring skirts), and a cream-colored blouse that hung on her two breasts as on two coat hangers. But her face was pale under its layer of makeup. Stains flowered over the skin of her face and over her neck. Like fragments of shadows tugging on her flesh. Within a few moments, even before deciding where to lay finally the handbag that swayed from side to side in her hand, she was already immersed, and I with her, in a raging sea of words, frothing with shame, confessions, pain, incitement. She said that she wants a shower, that she's tired, that she's had enough, that I never listen, that we've got to eat something, that my scarecrows are taking up more and more room and there's no space to move around in, that I never listen, that her throat hurts, that she saw a black cat, that I never listen, that she's frightened, that everything's getting more expensive, that it's been a wonderful day, that her aunt got a shock when she saw her, that the whole house is upside down, that I never listen when she talks.

I listened. I went on working, true, but what else could I do? What she actually meant to say was that I don't see her, that I don't look her in the eyes. She meant to say that I don't speak, that I don't participate in her conversation. That I don't participate with her.

But all at once I asked if anyone had been in the apartment. Perhaps I meant to ask about the strange fellow with the beard, the comb seller, who had said he would come and hadn't come. I asked about him from time to time, without thinking. It had become a habit. But that was enough for Batia. That was the signal.

Immediately she thought I was asking about Buki. Or she decided that I believed that that was what she would think, so she could launch into that flow of words, that ecstatic confession, so ridiculous and scorching, and, as I said above, shocking.

I already mentioned her ridiculous lovemaking with Buki, so we can skip most of her pathetic speech, and come directly to the shattering revelation that set off the real alarm in Naphtali, alerting him, weighing him down, maddening him, breaking into his being, which till then had been full to overflowing with noble thoughts of his taxidermy and visions and Lysanda. Batia continued:

"No. Buki didn't hate you at all. He envied you. He worshipped you. He talked about you so much. He used to say that you have great potential and it's a pity you're letting yourself fall apart. Your talent, he used to say, 'Naphtali's talent is fantastic. But he's losing touch with reality.' That's what Buki said. You need a woman, he said. Women are real, he said, are you listening? Yes. That's what he said. He was lying on his back, pleased with himself and with me. He went on talking about you with envy, hero-worship even, till I started getting a bit curious about you. Very curious, in fact. More fool I. And Buki lay there on his back full of satisfaction. It made me sick. All men make me sick when they're satisfied. But you were hungry, you're always hungry behind that calm, round moon-face of yours. Maybe that's what made me moonstruck. I wanted to wrap you up, to swaddle you in me, till you forgot the hunger, do you hear, till you forgot your hunger and found me everywhere. Everywhere. I was a fool, a fool. You remained hungry, and I—I got dizzy.

"Oh, my head, my head—never mind. It'll pass. Everything passes. I want you to know everything. So—yes, Buki. Buki used to say, 'I wonder what Naphtali Noi is doing now, in his loneliness. Thinking about a woman? Nonsense. If he is thinking about a woman, then it's about one that hasn't been born yet. It's possible that now Naphtali Noi is developing a new thesis in that sharp mind of his: that, say, one can, in one's thoughts, be in many places at once, and so why should one bother to move around? And that's just how he'd think about a woman,' too. I remember his words, because he used to repeat them so many times that they exhausted me and I thought to myself that if I go to Naphtali, all the spirits will flee his roof and he'll be mine, all mine. For what does a man need?—A woman. It's only if he has no woman that he invents spirits. And I could see my Naphtali suffering, in agony, with no one to look after him, going around like a bum, forgetting to eat his meals. And who but I, do you hear, I, who have suffered so much and have so much love to give, who but I, who am bursting with love, who but I could give him such true love, such great, frank, honest love, who but I could make him a nest to live in with security, honor, peace? Are you listening?

"Yes. I think you've started to listen. You're even smiling. Your hands are down and your cheeks have swollen in an evil, wicked smile. I can see right into your thoughts. Me and my spirits and Buki the famous ladies' man, and I took her from him, just like that, without any effort. What's that—pride? That's not very nice. Really, it doesn't suit you at all. Leave the pride to the poor bastards down there. I'll let you in on a secret, and it'll be the shock of your life.

You didn't take me from Buki. Buki, you hear, Buki sent me to you. What've you got to say now? Nothing, eh? Sure. But your mouth's all shrunk up around your pipe. And your hands have shot up into the air. But they'll stay there, I'm sure. You won't raise your hands to me even when I tell you that Buki sent me to share your bed with you, to put it as nicely as I can. What a fool I was. I came. No. I ran to you.

"Buki asked me: 'You won't be unfaithful to me, even with Naphtali Noi, will you?' I lied to him: 'Of course not.' Then he sent me to you, to ask for a rare book. You remember. Then I found out that he hadn't even looked at the book I brought back. I asked him, 'Why did you really send me?' He said, 'I wanted to know how he lives.' I said, 'What else?' He said, 'And so on.' I said, 'And so on what?' He said, 'I don't know myself.' I said to him, 'You, Buki, you who weigh every word, you didn't know?' He told me, 'Maybe I did know and I've forgotten.' I said to him, 'Try to remember.' He said, 'One doesn't have to tell everything one thinks.' I said, 'If you don't tell me then this is the last word we'll say to each other.' He said, 'I wanted him to have a woman.' I said, 'You wanted me to be his mistress.' He said, 'God forbid.' I said, 'Then you wanted him to love me so that he would envy you.' He said, 'Yes, yes.' That's what he said, the worm, the liar. So I said, 'That means you meant me to be mistress to both of you.' He said, 'No, no.' I said, 'What do you mean, no, no. Not to him or not to you?' He said, 'No, no,' and embraced and kissed me, the clever rat, and thought I wouldn't understand from what he said that he wanted to bring you down to his level, to be your partner, so that you'd become dependent on him, on him, when he isn't even good enough to kiss the little toe on one of your two white feet. He thought he'd be able to use you like a light switch, to turn you on and off as he pleased. And I was supposed to be the switch, operated by his handsome, masculine hands. Oh, Naphtali, my friend. You remember how I came to you—"

Allow me to stop here. The same sense of sinking, of irritation, overcomes me again in writing these words, as it did then. Oh, good people (I hope that at least one police officer and one police inspector will read these pages)—you surely expected that I would finally take this burning pipe out of my mouth and stuff it along with its smoldering tobacco into the devilish jaw of that Jezebel; or that at least I would throw her out, helping her to descend from my roof with a shove that would set her rolling down the sixty-five steps that lead to the earth, to the street, to the sewer, to her Buki with his "handsome, masculine hands"; or perhaps that I would stuff her, like a bird. I would fill her with sawdust (according to the instructions of Sternik, my teacher)—not with seaweed—as I do with my glorious birds—glorious, though unfinished. Oh, yes—unfinished!

Good people! All I can do now is to ask you to hold back your great contempt. And perhaps to light a candle. Please, respected policemen, when you read these pages—the writings of a man who no longer hopes for anything—read them by the light of a candle. For here is what I did to Batia: I embraced her. Yes, I embraced her, caressed her, petted her. And I almost cried. This is how it went:

(Batia continued) "And I was supposed to be the switch, operated by his handsome, masculine hands. Oh, Naphtali, my friend. You remember how I came to you with that book by—what's his name—"

"Kierkegaard," said Naphtali, and quickly shut his mouth as if wanting to pull the word back.

"Yes, Kierkegaard. That's right. You're listening, Naphtali. I knew you were listening. And I asked you if all his suffering was because he loved Regina so much, and you said, 'Yes. He loved her to the very limit of self-sacrifice.' "

"I said," said Naphtali, taking the pipe out of his mouth. Always the same mistake. She always makes the same mistake. "I said that he loved not her, but through her."

"Yes, that's right; and you said that Kierkegaard said that great love demands sacrifice."

"I said that Kierkegaard said that love consumes the lovers." He chopped out his words as if he were chewing gravel.

"Yes, till death," she said. "Till death. At that moment I felt that if a sacrifice was needed, then this roof was the most suitable place for it. I couldn't speak. I could feel my heart beating in my legs, my throat, in all my body, everywhere. From that moment I was lost and happy. It sounds funny, I know. But believe me, Naphtali, it's the greatest thing that ever happened to me. And now I'm tired, tired."

She cried. Her full body shook heavily, helplessly, as if everything in it had been exhausted, and rough streaks of color rolled down her face. They made her amazingly ugly, dirty, like a clown. The stains sharpened her edges, her chin grew smaller, her lips spread outward and pursed inward.

Naphtali held her hand. "Don't cry," he told her, "don't cry." Her big bust seemed to be trying to hide, to shrink inward, but it could not. They went inside and Batia fell onto the bed. Naphtali sat next to her and patted her on the back. Her skin was soft now. How had the tears reached that far? All the hardness of her skin seemed to have thawed. Naphtali caressed her back and her neck. Batia laid her head in his lap. "Your hand is hard," she said into his stomach, "you work hard," she said between sobs, as if that was what she really wanted to say to him. "Hold me tight," she added. He held her tight and caressed her back, her breasts, her lips, her thighs. They met him like old friends—with excitement, with a little leap. "Hold me tight, tight," she said. Her weeping was no longer helpless. And her body, in every place touched by his hand, his chest, his lips, filled with a new strength—actually, the old strength—and swelled up against him.

This contact with a life he could not control annoyed Naphtali. You must rest, he told her.

"Don't go!" She said. He did not go, but his hands were already gone. They floated above her body. "I'll bring you your pills," he said. "You've got to watch yourself."

"No," she said, with a fresh outburst of tears. He tried to get up and sat down. Again he tried to get up, upset.

"Now your man is getting up," said Naphtali as he got up, "and is going to bring you your pills. And you've got to rest. To have a good, long rest. And your man has to go. What did I want to say? Yes. Your man has got to put on his shoes. Because if your man goes out into the street without shoes everyone will laugh at him. Like, for example, a left shoe isn't a right shoe, and the other way around. But your man will come back, of course. So what did I want to say—the street. The street is near and far. So why am I going out into the street? Yes, your man is going out into the street to bring you some nice things. I'll bring you a doll in a scarf of silver stars and we'll call her Lysan—Lys—Lysandrella. Hell, whenever I put on this shirt it loses a button. Never mind, we'll put on the black shirt. Today's

Wednesday, the fourth day, I'll shake the sleeve and the moon will come out. It's late, it's already half past six. I've got to hurry to the newspaper."

XIX

I found myself in a mischievous mood. At the newspaper everyone laughed. I had never been so amusing. I'm a fairly serious person, short but quite stocky and as Batia put it (in Buki's words)—I don't like to move around too much. But that evening (the last one!) I was brisk and agile and worked like a demon. Trains, whole trains of words passed under my eyes. Underground trains. The entire print shop is doubtless made up of a network of underground passages, and even the neon there only deepens their darkness. I told them that. I felt light and free, like a man who finally knows that this is it. The compositors laughed. I told them that they were miners, and I wound my shirt around my head and tied it on my forehead like a miner's safety helmet with a torch. His highness the foreman, always gloomy, was angry that I was distracting the compositors from their work, but afterward he also laughed, though reluctantly. For I told them that they were moles, and I took off a shoe and showed them how a mole scratches, rubbing the end of my chin rapidly with the sole of my foot. Actually the sole of my foot was itching, but before this I had never taken off my shoe in public to scratch it. I was really amusing and sociable. And even with all that I did my work properly. Only once, or perhaps twice, did a bright green light appear in the wrong place on the rails and the train of words plunge off and explode.

On the way home I had a strange vision, as if I was peeling off my shadow, as if I could see my shadow moving away from me. It was on the corner of the streets that turn, one toward the beautiful Anath's glass verandah, and the other, through narrow lanes, to Leah's room. The road had been repaired and tarred, and the crossing was marked with cat's-eyes, and I really enjoyed walking across. I was certain that even on rainy days, slimy deep waters no longer filled this road. I walked across, light as a smile, and then I saw my shadow passing and continuing along the road to Anath's house. And the street, in which cars were passing and people were walking below lighted windows, suddenly seemed to me to be empty, very empty, verandahs hanging on the foreheads of houses, empty verandahs, and behind them square shutters.

I went into a small bar. This restored my spirits. Partly thanks to the brandy, but largely thanks to the barman. The walls were painted with naked Eves, flowers, snakes, and fig leaves, and the barman spoke to me in praise of faith. "It's like this," he said to me. "There's guys who believe in the evil eye, there's guys who believe in cards, and guys who believe in luck. You don't believe in anything, mister?" I believed him, and told him so. He poured me a glass. I began to like this man and wanted to say something good to him in return. I pointed to the bald heads and the flowering Eves and said to him that in the true Garden of Eden, the flowers grew straight out of the people's heads. I could see that my words made a strong impression on him, for he looked at me with eyes huge.

It was already after midnight, and the moon, having crossed the frontier of midnight, had begun blowing out puffs of mist, as light as smiles. Naphtali looked up, also light, light on his feet, like someone whose feet are borne by the inspiration to act. He climbed the steps in darkness, so that the light would not distract him, and as soon as he stepped onto his roof he knew that she was there, bundled up in the corner of shadow that the awning cast in the moonlight.

He opened the door to his room carefully, and without switching on the light, tiptoed across to the kitchen.

"Are you there, Naphtali?" He heard Batia's voice in her sleep.

"I'm here," Naphtali whispered, and took the square bottle of Cointreau out of its hiding place. He heard Batia's breath stop for a moment and then return to the quick, mad rhythm of the world of dreams.

"I'm here," he smiled mockingly, and sneaked back out onto the roof—he and a friendly shadow and the burning brandy between his fingers (because actually, the Cointreau was all finished a long time ago), closing the door cautiously on Batia's breathing and on Batia. Then he poured two glasses, downed the first in one gulp and spread the wings of his nostrils to expel the scalding gasp that then flooded his body. He poured another and gulped it down on top of the first, to catch the first up in the second and dissolve it deep in his blood. Then he wiped his mouth and looked at Lysanda's full glass. There was a white gleam on its face. He filled his own glass a third time and said, "L'chaim!"

And as he was raising the glass from the table, the white gleam leaped up and moved to and fro, as if Lysanda's lips had touched it.

"L'chaim," said Lysanda.

The moon donned a hat and puffed out its coiling wreaths of mist, its face swollen with satiation. Disgraceful! He wanted to shout to the moon: "Get off my roof!" But he was ashamed to do it in front of Lysanda, who was hiding in the shadows. And to give himself spirit, he threw the contents of her glass down his throat and his ears expanded and listened. "I knew you'd come back to me," said Lysanda. "Yes," he said. He heard the ripple of her gown as she moved from side to side on her seat, and her voice was like velvet upholstery. "Come out of the shadows, Lysanda." Instead of answering she laughed, and her laughter reverberated as in a crystal glass.

"Come out into the light, Lysanda."

"I'm scared," she said.

"Where have you been all this time, Lysanda?"

"By your side," she said.

"Were you jealous of Batia, Lysanda?"

She laughed.

"Why are you laughing, Lysanda?"

"I knew you'd come back to me," she said.

"How did you know, Lysanda?"

"Both of us knew," she said.

"Conceited!" he called.

She laughed.

"Come out into the light, Lysanda."

"I'll come out into *your* light," she said.

He went up to his toolbox and opened it. Inside it were seaweed, nylon skin, saucers of paint and glue, springy steel wire, and feathers. Plenty of feathers. Some that had been left over from birds he had stuffed, and some that he had collected. Gray feathers and colored feathers. When his hand touched them, they breathed. And in among them was a long bag, and in the bag—candles. In the flame of the candles he would do fine lead soldering, and with the wax he would fill in cracks and crevices.

He took out a candle and stuck it into a little copper holder that he then put on top of a box. Then he straightened out the wick and lit it with a match. He stood up, bent down his head, and passed his two hands over the flame. The flame settled down into the wax, melting a few drops, and then blazed up with a flash, sending up a feather of smoke, rising blue, assured and wonderful, like a citron illumined from within. Then he passed his outstretched palms over it in two opposing circles, and saw how the shadows separated and fled. This is my light. "Where are you, Lysanda?"

"I'm here," she said. Her voice rang out from the jasmine shrub. He looked at the jasmine shrub that till then had been flowerless and thin—for several weeks he had not attended to it properly—but now had sent forth blossoms, like tiny tongues. Lysanda was not there. She laughed from by the bougainvillea, covering her face with one of its branches. He looked at the bougainvillea. One of its branches was moving, but Lysanda wasn't there, she was already laughing from somewhere else, in fact she was laughing from a number of places at once.

He paced slowly, candle in hand, and surveyed his taxidermy (how I hate that word: "stuffing." A crude, nauseating sound; good enough for Sternik perhaps. Whenever I say *stuffing*, something cuts through to the depth of Naphtali's romantic soul, an echo, a better term, something with grandeur, beauty, enchantment like naphtoloides—naphtilides—phtylides—phtylyandes—phtyly-sandes—). The roof was drunk with moonlight, and his creatures, washed in the dull gleam, wavered slightly. Their rough joints, seams, and gluings could no longer be seen. Good, Lysanda's fingers caressed them. He would call her and she would come out to him.

Like one who delays his delight in order to enhance it, he went on preparing himself fastidiously. Out of the toolbox he pulled a gray, prickly Arab robe, which he had bought on one of his trips and had only worn once, as a carnival costume on Purim.

He put it on now and tied a brown rope around his waist. Then he placed a mirror in front of his face, and by the light of the candle messed and tangled his hair; he took a paintbrush, dipped it in dark brown paint and continued the line of the eyebrows around his eyes; he fixed his mouth by painting a line above his lips and another one below them—both of them reaching from ear to ear—and joined them to each other with straight lines. "Dance, Lysanda," he cried.

Lysanda danced. And Naphtali Noi, the sole master of this primeval empire, calmly put his tools back into his box and lit his pipe with a suitably ritualized gesture. He took the candleholder in the palm of his hand, placed it on the floor in the center of the roof, put a piece of kindling into the flame till it too caught fire, lit his pipe with the burning piece of kindling and with long, deep puffs, sent circles of aromatic smoke swirling hither and thither. Then he sat down, poured himself a glass, and sent its contents down to rest beside its predecessors. They met each other with love inside him. "That's nice, Lysanda, yes, Lysanda, go on, Lysanda."

How shall I describe Lysanda? How shall I describe this rebellious daughter of my blazing imagination, this creature of my loneliness and fear, the princess of my dreams, a thousand faces and a single essence? Oh, words, sententious, treacherous words—what shall I do with you? Cut out my tongue, hangmen, find me a new tongue, poets, a new language, with no words, no voices, no voice, a language of dust and wind—Lysanda! Anath's bright, dark face, the color of rice and shimmering grain, dreamy eyes radiating warm mist like a cot, but God, please, not with her sharp little nose jutting out so unbearably straight, I'll press in your nose a bit so it won't jut out so repulsively . . . Sit down in the sun like a little animal—naked, brown, tanned—lick your lapping tongue over that little stain on your right thigh while a shady trail of salt quivers along your spine and melts Naphtali's dry tongue in turn . . . Come up out of the anthropology books with huge conical nipples and burst into a wild breast-dance of adoration for your lord and maker who sits here on a low stool with his pipe swinging between his teeth in never-ending love and hangs copper bells on the pale pink nipples of your breasts . . . Lash your flowing hair over your thighs like whips woven by the hands of your cruel master, who laps up the wonder of your curving flesh in helpless passion . . . Press your precious, cool, slender neck to the goatish forehead (in its scholarly disguise) of your lord, while the broad back and close-cropped hair of the good Batia seek, in stubborn generosity, the kisses of his weary lips . . . Melt, with your soft, lilac-scented breath, the sounds arising from Batia's sleep and imparting, in all their earthy candor, the tastes of the dishes of our last humble meal. Feverish imagination. The final fluttering of a dying memory.

Now she was different. Days, weeks, of monastic seclusion with his stuffed animals had prepared him for this. He almost didn't need his senses to detect her—his vision to see her, his touch to feel her breath, his hearing to listen to the tapping of her feet in her strange rhythmic dance that had motion but no movement, silence but no rest. How to describe this dance?

How to describe Lysanda's dance? How to describe this dance, which first fired a flush through Naphtali's flesh and then slowly took from him all sense of his body and left him a pair of transparent wings without a head, without legs (and, as it later turned out, with a ravenous beak) fluttering above the abyss. How to describe this coiling wave that surged from transparent fingertips through arms to shoulders, this fan of hair so dizzily flapping, this motion of clinging knees like twin pomegranates swinging from side to side, accompanied by the motion of Naphtali's pipe, precise and unconscious, like the motion of stillness!

How to describe the way Lysanda, the child of my soul, was struck down, and almost collapsed in her execution of this all-dimensional exercise by a nasal snore, innocent but loud and obstinate, which escaped from Batia's deep dream, plowed through the closed door, and reverberated between her dancing feet. What could Naphtali do! He gulped down a quick glass of encouragement and clenched his eyes shut to bring back Lysanda's dance in all its original splendor. His hands were still, his pipe shuddered, his thighs were still. They waited. Then he felt the touch of Lysanda's hand. It was resting on his shoulder. He had never felt her as close as this. His shoulder reached after the touch of her hand, as if enchanted. He got up and followed her hand, and bent down to the candle and put the candleholder with the burning candle on the palm of his outstretched hand.

Silently he opened the door inside, and the door opened silently (good, exacting Batia, who was always so careful, had oiled the hinges), covering the flame with the closed fingers of his free hand. Shadows separated out of the darkness and fled in panic to the walls. He opened his fingers a little and cast strips of light onto the bed where Batia lay asleep.

Batia's sleep was deep and heavy. She lay on her back in a peace that was heartrending. A broad peace filled the whole bed. Her breasts, which had slipped out of her brassiere, flowed to the sides like tendrils spreading from a bared root. Her flabby biceps, folds of flesh, all seemed to express a desire to expand, to absorb, to swell. She lay there, a wife for a man, a mother for children, a good piece of earth, fertile.

Suddenly he saw that she was looking at him. Her eyes torn wide open, stricken with horror, looking for something on his shaggy robe. Naphtali moved his free hand away from the candle so that Batia could see better. The full candlelight cast a nervous flush over Batia's face and two red roses seemed to blossom in her cheeks.

It was a wonderful sight. He had never seen her like this. Slowly he raised the candle to his face. Her face lit up for a moment as if recognizing something in the extinguished pipe that was stuck between his two rows of teeth. She raised her head and shook it about wildly, opening her mouth wide to say something, perhaps to scream. But her head fell back onto the pillow and the scream stayed inside. A mighty yellow, like the color of dough, spread across her face, her forehead, her neck. That firm chin of hers was lying there now like something abandoned. Her bosom was very still. A noble nipple lay at rest at some distance from her body. He expected it to bud out into a red flower, but it didn't. Naphtali's sensitive eyes hurt. It doesn't matter, he consoled himself, I can fix her looks up later, with the right materials. I wonder if her last words, had they been heard, were words of love, he thought. Then he whispered sadly, "Lysanda."

But Lysanda did not answer.

She's hiding, the naughty thing, thought Naphtali. A sharp pain seared his shoulder, the shoulder on which Lysanda's hand had rested, and where he no longer felt the touch of her hand. Little lead soldiers now came scurrying over to his feet.

"Lysanda!" he shouted aloud. His voice melted away without an echo and a great dread brought back the sense to his knees, his kidneys, his heart, his head. He turned around—no Lysanda. Wretched shadows rustled in the comers. He whispered, "Lysanda, come to me." He dragged his feet out onto the roof: "Lysanda." The chill of dawn cloaked the outside. Dew dripped down his stuffed animals, those miserable, squashed stuffed heaps of open seams and torn wings, beginnings that had not been completed, that would never be completed. His feet slipped on the mounds of tar.

"Lysanda," he whispered voicelessly, helplessly, hopelessly, and dragged his feet back inside.

The candle fell from his hand, flickered on the floor and went out. Naphtali slowly took off the robe and laid it over the corpse, which now looked into his eyes—eyes that refused to face the morning—like Lysanda's corpse—*Lysanda dead*—a pile of gleaming copper hair spread over her chest, still as a seashell. Then he dragged himself to the corner of the room, tucked himself into his own stomach, and lay there.

XX

I have written a poem. After everything else, that sounds ridiculous, I know. But it's a fact.

As soon as I got up (it was already noon), I knew I wouldn't be able to do anything else. I took a piece of paper and filled it with nice musical lines. Possibly it's more of a song than a poem. The toolbox was far away from me and I barely had the strength to hold a pen, let alone a hammer. Lysanda's death was so beautiful.

In fact, the beauty of death is greater than any other beauty, and of course a beautiful death is much better than a crude one. I know this is not well put. I'll explain. The death of Mrs. Kapusta, for example, only filled me with disgust. Whereas I almost burst into tears on seeing Juliet dying on the stage. That was divine. But I wrote no poem then. My hands did not hurt then, apart from the usual pain of creation. And so I built a wondrous creature instead. One that has no name. But I made it of such a pure framework of lines that the seaweed, the plastic skin, the steel wire, the seams, the glue, and all the other materials were almost unnoticeable. And perhaps I did not make this creature at all, except in my imagination. My memory is so muddled.

Maybe it isn't exactly a poem, these verses I have written. But this I swear—that it revived me like a strong drug, like the last cigarette of a man condemned to death. Ah yes—death again.

Of course, I knew this was the last thing I would do, like the last flutter of a bird with the hunter's bullet in its heart (forgive the emotion). I shoved the page with the poem—or perhaps ballad—deep into the pocket of my shirt—one of the four pockets of my orange shirt that I used to fill with sweets and sometimes with toys whenever I went down to my little beauties Nili and Lili.

I went down to my little beauties, of course. As soon as I heard (through the drainpipe in the bathroom) the sleep-thick voice of Mr. Schturz, yawning as he said good-bye to his family, I went down to them. And my little ones, whom I had neglected of late, no longer twittered to me in their darling voices ("Come Yakoko, come on to us Yakoko," and so on), but I came to them dragging my feet (when had I eaten last?). Mrs. Schturz vanished in a flash, and the little ones, whose sharp eyes immediately noticed my weak state, began kicking me with their little feet, rolling me over on the carpet, throwing their nimble hands at my face in glorious mirth, pelting me with the pits of olives and peaches—the remnants of their afternoon meal, which Mrs. Schturz had not had time to clear away before she rushed off. And the little ones danced around me and sang:

"Yakoko my koko
Go get us some choko
Yah kee yah koko
Yah koko riko"

Then they suddenly grew serious and commanded me to crawl from one to the other to try to catch them—little balls of fire—until my pockets were empty and the sweets were scattered all over the room. I sat like a discarded steak on the carpet.

"Why is she like that?" asked Nili, and looked at the doll with the plait. "Why is she sad?" asked Lili, and also looked at the doll.

"Yakoko bad boy," said Nili, and Lili said, "You're dead. Mama said you don't come 'cos maybe you're dead like Kapusta."

I shut my eyes and pretended to be dead. I could have stayed there like that. Actually I don't know a better place. But Nili and Lili ordered me to get up and tell them the story of the witch.

They sat me down on a chair. I sat down. My two little demons sat down on my knees. Nili on the right knee and Lili on the left knee. I told them about the King who never laughs and about the shepherd girl, who tells him of the beautiful maiden in the cave, and about the witch that is brought before the king and promises him that she will give him the maiden his heart desires at one minute after midnight, on condition that he sets a room aside for her, with a mirror and a candle, and the king promises her all this, and also swears that he will not touch the maiden, and all the people of the city mass around the windows of the palace, the shepherd girl among them. And at one minute after midnight the king goes into the witch's room, and whom does he find facing the mirror by the light of the candle—

"The beautiful maiden," says Nili gravely.

"The beautiful maiden," says Lili.

"But where's the witch?" asks Nili.

"Tell us about the witch," pleaded Lili.

And I tell them how the king's heart ached when he saw the maiden of his dreams and he forgot his oath and touched the maiden, just barely touched the maiden, and then—

"And then the witch came," my little demons jumped gleefully up and down on my knees.

"No," I said. "She went up into the sky. The beautiful maiden went up into the sky through the chimney."

"And what happened to the king?" asked my little ones.

"The king went up after her," I said.

"So she was a witch," said Nili reluctantly.

"So she was a witch," said Lili.

"Yes," I said. "And all the people of the city went up after the king."

"And no one at all remained in the city?" asked my little ones.

"Only the shepherd girl," I said. "And she went back to the forest."

"Tell us about the witch," said Nili.

"Yes, tell us," Lili repeated.

I dragged my legs apart. I was very tired. I took out the piece of paper from deep down in my pocket, straightened it out between my hands, and read:

The sky above loves Lysanda
The sky embraces Lysanda
Hallelujah.
All the city loved Lysanda
All the city followed Lysanda
As she rose from the chimney with a wail
Into the midnight's veil.

He came to the empty city—
Lysanda!
Seeking the oracle of the caves—

Lysanda!
Then he caroused with skulls and with stones
And tickled the walls till they laughed
And burned all the city with plague and with song—
Hallelujah.

I did not cry. This was my poem. I called it "Elegy on the Death of Lysanda." The lines twitched before my eyes, the letters scattered. Like at the newspaper, at times, when I get tired. I was very tired. Nili and Lili moved away from me, flew away from me like two winged demons. Where to? To the door.

And in the doorway stood all the tenants of the house, Mr. Schturz at the head, with a policeman next to him. And around them and behind them: Mrs. Schturz, Mr. Rabman and his wife, Mr. Gross, Mr. Paldi, Mr. Rockman, and their wives, Mr. Getz, Mr. Gurfink, Mr. Zabman, and their wives—all the tenants of the house. Nili and Lili embraced the stout legs of Mrs. Schturz and Mr. Schturz and clung to them. They looked at me with a queer strangeness, perhaps even with terror. The others also looked at me with strangeness, but not without curiosity. On the wall opposite me hung an old clock with huge hands and blurred numbers. I took the opportunity of finding everybody together here, hardened my weakened voice as much as I could, and, raising my hands, one toward the clock and the other toward the doorway, said:

Don't tell the children the death of Lysanda!
Cover the children's heads!
Stop all the clocks!

The fleshy hands of Mrs. Schturz spread themselves over the little girls' heads, and the hands of Mr. Schturz pointed at me: "He broke the light switch on the staircase," he said.

"On purpose," said Mr. Zabman.

"We warned him from the start," said Mrs. Gurfink.

"Yes, yes," said the tenants.

"He has no consideration for others at all," said Mrs. Rockman.

"Mrs. Fleischman sprained her leg—Mrs. Fleischman's my cousin—because it was dark on the staircase," said Mrs. Schturz.

"Yes, yes," said the tenants.

"Take him away, constable," said Mr. Schturz.

The policeman bowed and smiled at me pleasantly. "Come with me," he said. A vast dread encompassed his smiling face. He looked like the comb vendor. Perhaps he was the comb vendor. The old clock on the wall ticked like the sounds of a train that passed a long time ago. He had finally come for me. I returned his bow and invited him up to my roof. But my legs had already started to die. Somehow I dragged myself after him.

ANTS

TRANSLATED BY DAVID ZARAF

Chapter I

Slight postponement of a divorce—The Ledger and the Book—
An original way of celebrating the Sabbath—An ant excites my wife,
and I take revenge on the ant.

We decided to divorce. I knew for some time that we'd have to do it. My wife never actually said "yes" in so many words, but when I said "Come," she was already dressed and ready to go.

It was difficult to explain why to the rabbi. A man goes to the doctor with a fly buzzing in his ear, and the second he arrives the buzzing stops. Our apartment is small, one room and some space on the roof, and we run into each other a lot and so get embarrassed a lot. If my wife was like other women, she'd have children. But my wife doesn't let me have my way with her like a man has with a woman. I'm a first-class builder; I can split a scaffolding plank with my bare hands if it's necessary. But I can't handle Rachel roughly. What a wonderful flower the calla lily is. It's a flower I've always been afraid to touch. White as snow, noble, unaffected by sun or rain. Rachel has a proud bearing, a soft gait, and brown hair that she pins up on the back of her head. Her body is white, as white as alabaster. She can lie in the sun for hours and her body will remain as white as it was before she lay down.

The rabbi waited. Neither of us knew what to say. Suddenly I stood up, went to my wife, and pressed my lips against hers. She bit my lips till they bled, my wife did. Then she spit into a snow-white handkerchief with which she then wiped her lips.

The rabbi asked Rachel if I disgusted her. She answered, "Not particularly." He asked her if she loved me, and she again answered, "Not particularly." He asked her if she had loved other men before me, and she said she didn't remember. Her expression was innocent and open. Once, while she was answering the rabbi, she rubbed under her breast, with her long, beautiful fingers, as though she had an itch. After we left the rabbi's office, I asked her why she had made such a rude gesture in his presence. She had felt, she said, as though ants were crawling over her body. The rabbi told us to come back in two months' time. Meanwhile, he advised, we should think of changing apartments.

"Change your place, change your luck," the rabbi said.

The idea of changing apartments took hold of me. To build a house, a home for Rachel and me. Perhaps a new house would mean a new start. And after all, building is what I do.

As soon as we got home, I went to the calendar that hangs in our little kitchen, turned over a few leaves, and on a suitable date after waving away a little ant that was scurrying across the day I had selected I wrote the words, "New House." The letters were clear and carefully shaped, with a heavy line under the word "New." Above was colored landscape—all the calendar pages had colored landscapes of historical sites—a rock fortress with ancient stone walls at the top that had been burned and had now been restored. I told my wife that I was going to build a house for us. "Good," she said, and she looked the other way.

Now that I was about to build a new house for us, it became easier to put up with the shortcomings of our old one. Our apartment was small, on the top floor of an old house, with a small living room and a hall. The hall lead into the main room, the main room lead into a tiny kitchen, the tiny kitchen into a very small washroom, where the shower—there is no bathtub—and the toilet stand close together. All the doors run in a straight line from the door to the roof, and we can't help bumping into each other again and again. It's embarrassing. When we were first married, Rachel would giggle and then escape. Now she scratches, not ungracefully, under her arm, between her breasts, or just above her belly—and hurries to the shower. If I suddenly embrace her, the sound of her laughter rings out magnificently until I let her go, but it is laughter as cold as glass.

At night Rachel wraps herself in the sheets, and looks like a statue draped within them. White, impervious stone.

The house is always very clean. When I come home from work, I undress outside on the roof and go to the shower in slippers.

When I want to lie down she lays a coarse cover over the green bedspread. When I want to lean my elbows on the table, she says, "Excuse me," and spreads a gray but clean napkin under my elbows. She serves our meals dressed in a white smock, like a nurse's, and after we've eaten and I want to hold her hand, she escapes into the shower. I wash the dishes and listen to the water in the shower running down and caressing her body. Once I asked her why she showers so often. "The house is crawling," she answered. I heard the budding of a strange, suppressed laughter in her voice.

I can of course keep myself busy in other ways, for instance with my accounts. I'm careful about the ledger—that's a matter of business. But it's enough if I add it up and balance it on Saturday mornings. The rest of the week I open it when I come home from work just to enter, in carefully shaped letters, a line or two of expenses for building materials, wages, and so forth. I hardly ever read books. I think I've lost the taste for reading as entertainment. Sometimes I look at the newspaper during lunch on a building site, when I eat the sandwiches that have been wrapped in it. Apart from that, I read the Book. I read it every Friday night after dinner, and sometimes on other nights, too, before going to bed. A matter of tradition. There was a time when I used to put my heart into it and read with devotion. Now I hear myself reading it out loud while I think about something else. Perhaps I am becoming lazy. I have never read the Book systematically, just a little here, a little there, where it happens to fall open. There is one place I read from often, because my wife likes to hear it, particularly on Friday night after dinner, when she lights a cigarette from the flame of the Sabbath candles. Sometimes I read it to her on other nights as well, in bed, when her eyes are closed. "Go on," she says, when I close the Book thinking she's fallen asleep.

"For a nation is come upon my land, strong, and without number, whose teeth are the teeth of a lion, and he hath the cheek teeth of a great lion." Here I stop, and my wife says "Go on," and I skip a bit and read, "Alas for the day! for the day of the Lord is at hand, and as a destruction from the Almighty shall it come."

Sometimes my wife stops me while I'm reading this part and says, "Tickle me!" Happily I put down, almost throw down the Book and draw my fingers along the soles of her feet, first one foot and then the other, so that my wife Rachel laughs. This is the closest contact there is between us. No wonder that my heart weeps inside of me when she laughs.

The tickling ceremony is our Sabbath pleasure. It tires us out. I fall asleep and dream that she-leopards are embracing me and scratching me with their claws; when I wake up, my wife Rachel is in the shower.

How much time does my wife Rachel spend in the shower? It varies. In the winter she dries her body by the fire of the stove; in the summer, by the heat of the sun. Many times I have asked my wife Rachel why she doesn't wipe down her body with a towel, and each time her answer is different. Once she answered from the sun-drenched roof: "Have you ever seen a tree or a bird towel itself?" Fascinated and full of admiration I stand and look at her nude, pulsating body. The virginal white burning with icy fire, she walks on the blazing roof as though she is floating, spreading and folding her arms, the water on her body dripping down in golden ribbons.

The Sabbath and its enjoyments were over. When I opened my eyes and was free of the she-leopards clawing their hot and pulsating bellies, I saw the milky light of the morning spilling through the window.

"To build us a house," I said to myself and got up from the bed. "I have to get up early to build us a new house."

Behind me, from the bed, there came noises of rustling and creaking. I turned my head and what did I see? My wife Rachel, with her eyes closed, throwing her head from side to side, her nostrils trembling, her thighs twitching, and her feet kicking. What has shaken her body so, what has taken it out of its glorious iciness?

A little ant, it seems, tiny, but full of energy; it had emerged from a fold in the sheet and onto the lower end of the curve of my wife Rachel's thigh. It climbed fast along the delicate curve and stopped there for a moment to raise its head and rub its antennae one against the other. I looked at the uncovered, sleeping bit of thigh where the ant had crossed, and an evil feeling welled up in my eyes and heart. For thirteen years I have constructed houses, hundreds of floors, thousands of tons of building material, and I have never succeeded in exciting my wife the way a little ant can.

The palm of my hand is big, crisscrossed with countless furrows from timber and steel and concrete, many furrows from very dead matter. I caught the ant between my finger and thumb and hurried to the roof. I rubbed my rough fingers over it, and what was left of it I crushed with my bare feet. As I did this, the tar of the roof showed from under the thin layer of whitewash, and on it—a trail of ants, dark as bronze grains, marching in slow procession to the front door.

Chapter II

Daily routine—Rachel and Bilha amuse themselves—
Strange noise.

Nothing special happened the next day. I worked harder, and I made my gang work harder, too, carried along by the exciting idea that it was our house I would be building—mine and Rachel's. Neither of us mentioned the visit to the rabbi. Actually we didn't talk much at all. Only once, almost incidentally, I hinted about the house I was going to build, and then I saw her eyes widening a little and the olive-green brown of her irises grew deeper.

This is how things went that day. I came home from work at half past four, and Rachel wasn't there. She was probably with her girlfriend—our neighbor Bilha. We have an unspoken agreement: when I come home from work, Rachel is at Bilha's. Pulling off boots, peeling off socks, rubbing sweat-caked feet, rolling my work clothes into a bundle of sour-salty smells—Rachel does not like to watch this. To tell the truth—I can't bear this routine either, not when Rachel is standing in front of me, all pure and clean. In our new house I'll have a special, screened-off corner for getting out of my work clothes. But for now, Rachel is at Bilha's, and I shave, shower, and lie down to sleep till about six.

That day, when I woke up from my siesta, a small chunk of mortar the size of a beetle was lying under my nose, exactly at the center of my moustache. This is Rachel's way telling me off for having accidentally carried two grains of sand or a little lump of mortar home from the scaffolding. I smiled. I didn't know which smell to concentrate on first in this little chunk of matter, that of Rachel's hand or of moist cement. I haven't said yet that on the way home, I had picked up the groceries, as I did every day, according to a list my wife had written.

Then supper, washing the dishes, a couple of chores around the house, a pipe—and the ledger. I am careful with my accounts, for my own wages depend on it, and those of the boys in my gang, too. Generally, Saturday morning is enough time for this. But now, since I have to keep my eyes wide open, so that I don't get too deep into debt, so that I can take on the expenses of building our new house, I have started looking it over on weekday evenings as well. Not that I have anything to enter or delete; everything was entered last Saturday. But I really had nothing else to do. Read the Book, you'll say; but that was something I couldn't do while Bilha was in our home. And Bilha was with us that evening (what evening wasn't she with us?)—very much with us.

They're laughing, the two of them. I am sitting at my desk in the hall and the door is open—and they're laughing. My wife Rachel's laughter is very fine, almost inaudible; Bilha's is heavy and dull. My wife is dressed in white; Bilha is in black. Bilha looks at me laughingly, and in her eyes Rachel is peering at me—that is how it feels. There are four corners in there and only one of them faces my seat in the hall. And that is the corner they've settled down in. I could have closed the door, but I was afraid that my wife would whisper into Bilha's ear and Bilha would say in an angry voice: "Keep it open, it's so stuffy in here." Bilha had put a restlessness in me; I had felt her knees under the table at suppertime. Bilha shared most of our meals with us—she cooked them—and she didn't really know what she was doing with her life, apart from helping Rachel.

Bilha on Rachel's knees. They were amusing themselves, or at least that was the way it looked in the darkness, behind the curling smoke of my pipe, out of the corner of my troubled eye. Their lips smacked, their tongues clicked. They passed a blue cup filled with fluffy custard from hand to hand. They licked the custard and extended syllables of pleasure poured out of their lips. Bilha knew how to prepare a thousand and one desserts that tasted of honey and Rachel liked them all—but, more than anything she loved real honey, bees' honey. "Want something nice?" Bilha called out to me, and Rachel's laughter rippled behind Bilha's back.

Then she looked at me over Bilha's shoulder. Her eyes were an olive-green, only lighter, much lighter. The eyes of the tigresses of my dreams. I spat out the last puff of my pipe before I extinguished it, and went out to the roof to look at the many houses, the twisting streets, the entrances to the buildings, the windows, to breathe the smell of flesh, the real smell. Something was bothering me.

At night, in the deep of the night, I can't say exactly at what hour, perhaps at two, or three, I woke up and heard a strange noise. I thought it was my imagination and I covered my ear to get rid of the noise. But the noise persisted. A kind of growling or dripping from deep down, but drier, like stones rolling, but duller, like what I used to hear long ago, as a child, when I would press my ear to the ground near the railroad tracks about fifteen minutes before the train pulled up. There were, of course, the street sounds of that hour: the rush of a passing car, a far-off cough, a laugh, a shutter being closed, a cat or a baby wailing, and all the rest, and the sound of the sea as well. And suddenly, very near, just under me, some man in the street calling, in a clear, exact, colorless, matter-of-fact voice—like someone shouting in broad daylight—"Yankele, come on now," and then someone named Yankele, passing by with a patter of footsteps, hurrying after the voice. I knew those sounds very well. Often enough I had run out to the roof, away from the torture of my bed, tired of circling again and again the white walls of my wife. There on the roof I stood listening to those sounds with closed eyes, and then I relaxed and fell asleep.

This sound was different. I remembered. Once I had heard a similar sound just before the collapse of a wing of a house in the Old City that we were repairing. I hadn't been in the wing that collapsed. I was in another part of the house at the time. But I could hear the sound. Millions and millions of grains of dust and stone moving from place to place . . . What a wonderful feeling.

Then silence. The noise had stopped. I went to the bathroom and rinsed out my ear. Then I sat down on the toilet seat and looked at a cockroach being given its funeral.

Chapter III

Ants dismember a half-dead cockroach—
Praise of the cockroach's antennae and of the beauty of its armor.

When I first saw them, busy, miserable little things whose length is measured in millimeters, gray, inflexible creatures with their bodies composed of round sections of which the smallest, such as the belly, are no larger than fly specks; when I first saw them milling around that brown, quivering mountain—the cockroach—it looked to me like a coronation or some other kind of ritual, centering on that rounded, exalted, and deeply sensitive entity. Soon I realized I was wrong: the ants were busy dismembering the cockroach.

Slowly, slowly they dissected it into sections. The cruel and disgusting aspect of it all was that that brown mountain was still alive. Turning the cockroach on its back (only the god of the ants knows how they managed that), they proceeded about their macabre business. Some seemed to be sucking its marrow, clamped to it as pincers, motionless, with the thrashings of the big body unable to dislodge them. I would long ago have made an end of this disgusting sight if my eye had not been drawn to the ants' careful handling of the cockroach's antennae. The antennae are no doubt the crowning glory of this most attractive species of insect: their antennae are very long, pliable, and extremely sensitive. One can easily imagine their being in great demand in Antland, perhaps as long-range communications devices. But the way the ants held on to them, God! What a ballet of forms and motion! It looked as if they were making a game of it, those little ants, until I wondered whether there was any truth in the legend of their efficiency, industriousness, and purposefulness, which even the Book helps to perpetuate.

One ant grabs the end of an antenna, which is perhaps a dozen times as long as itself or even more. And don't forget that even an ant is eight cubits long proportionally speaking. The antenna rises and waves of twisting tremors travel from its tip to its tail, which is held tightly between the sharp jaws of the ant. The ant pulls the antenna sideways, and not without considerable effort, as one may observe from the contortions of its own body, and the antenna follows along, as though surrendering, and slowly forms a perfectly arched rainbow. And just at the point where you would expect the bow to explode in a shower of colors or fitted with a deadly arrow, the antenna pulls free, lifts the ant into the air in a wide arc, straightens out in the air, and lands straight and smooth on the ground. And here's a wonder for you—the ant is still holding on there, at the end of the antenna, and is pulling on it once more.

I confess that; my jangled nerves didn't allow me to follow through and see just where this ugly, unjust, repeated, and unimaginative game of the ants would end. But from the industry that the little creatures exhibited in digging out the cockroach's eyes and sucking its tasty marrow, the results weren't hard to guess. Slowly the cockroach was emptied, like a barrel with open spigots. But what a barrel! A barrel made of rounded gold leaf, a kind of filigreed royal suit of armor—with nobody inside it—and I had to stand amazed at the sight of those antennae still having the strength to wave so majestically. And then you see that one of the golden sheets of the royal armor—what I would call the greave, for instance, of Goliath's plating, has already been dismantled completely. Let it be said to the praise of these disgusting ants that they preserve those treasures in their chambers, and also that they are careful about cleaning up the battlefield. By tomorrow, nothing will be left on the bathroom floor, neither of them nor of that glorious creature they have dismembered.

Not without disgust I took hold of one of those ugly angels of destruction between my thumb and forefinger and laid it on the drainboard in the kitchen, next to the cup of honey-flavored custard that Rachel and Bilha had left. Perhaps I intended to study the creature a little longer, through the magnifying glass that I still had from the days when I collected stamps. At any rate, I soon forgot about it and lay down to sleep beside Rachel, who was wrapped up in pure white sheets, ah, white as snow.

Chapter IV

Small-scale invasion of ants—I subdue them with boiling water
and poisons—I subdue my wife to my lust—A crack in the wall.

I had hardly returned from work when I heard Rachel's voice from
the darkness of the kitchen. She stood there, staring at the bottom
of a cup, tears running out of her eyes. A long, dense stream of ants
stretched from the cup to the tiled part of the wall—with barely
an opening in the wall to be seen. They marched in multi-lane
processions, an army of stippled lines, and they filled the bottom
of the cup. I understood that this was what pained my wife so: she
dearly loved the products of Bilha's culinary imagination.

But my wife Rachel was not exactly crying. There were big drops
of tears on her cheeks but her eyes were already dry. She stared.
Where did she stare? At what? What was on my wife's mind now?

There she stood, almost bending over, with her graceful hands
held out, as though she were defending herself, as if there were
some third being between us.

The next day I didn't go to work and waged war against the ants.
I thought them rather disgusting, and I wasn't reluctant to do
whatever was necessary to banish the plague from our home; I say

our home, for in the course of the extermination I discovered a few more of their hiding places: under the kitchen windowsill, around the door posts of the kitchen, at almost all the corners of the glazed tiles in the bathroom, and also one place in the main room, at the corner of a floor tile—I worked with boiling water. For several hours I treated the cracks to streams of boiling water. Here and there, a rustling started and in most cases spread from place to place. Quite a few corpses marked the trails now. Their inferior organizational skills now became evident: general confusion, running about in all directions at once, a hurried, graceless, even hysterical touching of one another as they collided in the haste of their escape. Still, they took pains to remove the cadavers of their comrades. To their larders or to their cemeteries, I cannot say. And yet, I must speak one word in their favor.

I operated of course in a logical manner, and now, as I review the maneuvers in this little campaign, I cannot help but confess that here and there my higher order of intelligence was impressed by their lower. For example, at the openings of the cracks. Perhaps they were just curious, perhaps they were sentries or lookouts—but they would not abandon their posts until the stream of boiling water caught them. And then, the rare lone individual soldiers. They may have been adventurers or scouts—could it be that some law of chivalry forbade them to disguise themselves as corpses? A few drops of boiling water were enough for those single drones, whose misfortune, or perhaps instructions, had put them in my path, on the wall, the drainboard, the floor, outside their hidden fortresses. In short, as that day drew to its end, I felt entitled to rub my hands together in pleasure. The drainboard, the tiles, the corners of the woodwork—all clear of ants, and the kitchen sink was full of them, heaps upon black heaps of little cadavers.

In light of my achievement there was, to say the least, something odd about my wife's reaction, she who had been dozing in the sun most of the day:

"Are you absolutely sure there aren't any left?"

The next day I worked with poison. That very same night, Rachel had stepped on some live ants. They were on their way from our living space to the little hall—straight through the door, the insolent creatures. Rachel jumped to her feet and giggled. What her laughter meant I couldn't say. I switched on all the lights in the house. The ants carried on their traffic as if nothing had happened, bypassing the site of the massacre, where some of them were still busy with what looked like corpse removal. That did not frighten me, though, to tell the truth, it made me a little ashamed: there was something stubborn, arrogant about their activities. I almost want to call it hubris. After all, it was obvious that they would seek new burrows after I had uprooted them from their old homes. That, at any rate, was something I could count as a success. A definite tactical victory.

I told Rachel so; she only nodded.

I didn't go to work the next day either, for I was determined to finish the job. Systematically I filled all the gaps and cracks—in short, anything that could have served as access to an ant nest. And I improved on my weapons as well as I could, putting down ingestion poisons and inhalation poisons in alternating layers.

Friday morning I ended the work of extermination, put the rest of the corpses in the garbage pail, checked all the weak spots once again to be on the safe side, and in my quiet, undemonstrative way, without a trace of conceit, informed my wife of the successful completion of my campaign.

Rachel nodded.

It was Sabbath eve. The night I had anxiously awaited and feared. I wanted to be worthy of it. I was happy that the ant plague had come my way toward the end of the week so that I could wipe it out and purify my home again. I was pleased that Bilha was ill and could not share our Sabbath meal. I saw it as a good omen. I deserved a greater share of this Sabbath than I had enjoyed on previous weekends. I was angry with Rachel for lighting a cigarette using the Sabbath candles and exhaling curls of smoke with closed eyes. But I didn't tell her so. After all, she does it every Sabbath and I never take offense. I didn't look her in the eyes. Rachel went to bed without asking me, as she did every Sabbath, to tickle the soles of her feet. Instead she lay down between the double, very white sheets, a queen in a palace of ice.

I picked up my ledger, but I didn't know what to do with it now. I hadn't been to work in three days, and I had no idea what money had come in and what had gone out, what to add and what to subtract from my accounts. I left the ledger go and opened the Book. I read from Genesis, and a joy bordering on jubilation filled my heart and crotch. I mounted my wife's bed completely naked and called solemnly, like a battle cry:

"Rachel, today our task is ended. Tonight you shall escape from your white sheets like a butterfly from its cocoon—and I will possess you!"

Rachel wrestled with me the greater part of the night and I wrestled with her and with her white sheets and then—her breath stopped, her lips clamped together, her hands pressed against her two breasts, and wrinkles furrowed her brow as I worked my will on her. Ah, the sleep of the shamed! I dreamed that I was crawling along on my six short legs with an empty glass in my mouth and I didn't know what to do with the glass and I was afraid that it would shatter in my mouth.

I woke to the sound of something cracking. I switched on the light and jumped off the bed. Rachel was on her knees, dripping with water, by the wall that adjoined the kitchen, her hands crossed over her chest and her eyes glued to said wall. About two and a half feet above the floor a crack had opened in the wall like a gaping sphincter, with ants gray as cement bricks marching in and out.

"Dragon's teeth," Rachel whispered and wouldn't look at me.

A long dull groan was rising out of the crack in the wall, which looked as if a row of four triangular teeth had bitten into it.

I fell into a sleep that was a bottomless pit.

Chapter V

*The honey trap—A new race of ants appears, hasty and strong—
Description of the mandibles and their many uses.*

I rose about noon and immediately sat down to work. I needed to put my little complaints to the side and bring order into the ledger, which for three or four days had been lying on my desk open to a half-balanced page. My attention had been lured away from it. I had no receipts or invoices for the last few days, and a man feeling his way in pitch darkness would have had an easier time of it than I, who ended up adding estimated figures in brackets only to save myself the shame. I know them, the men of my crew. They don't say a word, they draw silently on their cigarettes, and all they do is give me a sharp look between drags. I tried to settle my confused mind by smoking my pipe, and also by revenging myself a bit more on those little creatures, two or three of whose representatives were holding a little businesslike procession inside the brackets on the open page, feeling the figures here and there as if they were checking up on me. Into the glowing coal of my pipe I pushed their tiny bodies. I executed them by burning. Then I heard laughter from the kitchen, a kind of playful giggle. I recognized my wife's laugh. My wife was amusing herself. Rachel is inventive enough at amusing herself that I am often shocked at how little it takes. I approached on the tips of my bare toes—I had left my slippers beside my desk—and spied on her. A green curtain was spread across the kitchen doorway. I pressed my body to the wall and kept my eye at the opening in the curtain.

Two ants, one and then another, dropped at that very moment into a small, half-full jar of honey. They had seemed to appear from nowhere, or from the air itself. As the third one dropped into the jar, I raised my head and saw the fourth was detaching itself from the kitchen ceiling and quickly diving through two yards of air, straight into the jar of honey. And my wife, wrapped in a crocus-yellow flower-patterned dressing gown, stood there eating honey out of a small cup. I have already said that my wife Rachel likes honey—and the bowl of the spoon slid about above her tongue as she laughed in nonchalant self-indulgence.

In the course of observing this brief spectacle, a plan was being formulated in my brain. Two details of this tableau stood out to me, seeming particularly meaningful. First, the bottom part of the jar was immersed in a dish filled with water, and that was apparently the reason why those greedy ants had no alternative but to choose this roundabout means of raiding the honey; second, as they dropped to their destination, the ants enthusiastically furrowed their way into the soft honey and so, before dying, made certain there would be room for the ants that were to follow.

"Darling," I called to Rachel, "I have discovered the ultimate weapon!"

"Shshsh," Rachel gestured at me over the teaspoon as she saw me emerging from my hiding place behind the curtain. The laughter was around her eyes, and the eyes themselves were as a stream of congealed honey.

I decided to act quickly. I took all the jars of "Choice Honey" from Rachel's secret store and opened them. I poured the contents into every glass and cup and saucer and jar I could find in the house. Rachel, when she understood, also did her share enthusiastically, and placed the vessels more or less equidistant on the floor, on the armchair, on the table, approximately one container per square yard, with the bottom quarter of each of the containers immersed in a little bowl of water. I could, of course, have laid down the containers of honey without the bowls of water, but I did not do so for two reasons. First, without the water screen the ants would come the direct way, and then we would find the floor and the carpet and our few pieces of furniture and crockery and clothes all crawling. The method of honey jars protected by moats promised to be a "cleaner" method, with the formic launching pad thus confined to the ceiling only.

Second—and this was what convinced me—the indirect route was daring (a jump into space) and clever (circumventing an obstacle), which—probably—only the strong would attempt, so that the elite of the race would be annihilated; the weak remnants, having no leaders or guides, would degenerate and die by the thousands in their nests in the walls. This powerful and final justification I did not reveal to Rachel. Why, I do not know myself. Perhaps I simply felt it would be a bad idea—an intuition, from the heart.

It was a shocking and at the same time terrifying and majestic sight. The bright moonlight that flooded the ceiling through the upward slanting slants of the shutters and left us in the half-dark, my wife Rachel and I, each hunched on a different side of the bed, tensely expectant, revealed their activities. They didn't all come at once. Only some, perhaps the scouts, arrived from different directions at the same moment. They circled around, searching perhaps, made many sudden stops, groped about, then dispersed and disappeared.

But then the sound of their activities in the wall suddenly stopped, and a drawn-out groan, like a horn sounding, gradually replaced the gnawing noises. The cracks did not widen as the ants appeared in broad columns. First dives followed—trial dives into the gaping mouths of the jars, leaving almost no trace. The honey didn't even bubble at the touch of the tiny bodies.

I'm not clear on all the ways ants have to communicate, their communications media. I suppose that in addition to such ordinary means as light waves that are received through thousands of little eyes, sound and smell waves that are intercepted and broadcast through the appropriate sections of antennae, emergency measures such as warning, control, and coordination centers could be brought into action. But however much I focused my own senses, they did not perceive anything out of the ordinary. Thus, I am forced to indulge in suppositions, so as not to feel like a useless bystander among the giant procession lining up within the walls, moving in to the veins of the tunnels, suddenly revealing itself behind the cloud of dust from a cracking wall, and flowing between the patches of light on our ceiling. Multitudes of tiny ants, heads set between their antennae as if they cared only about what lay ahead, turning incessantly left and right as if repeating some secret handshake. Very possibly the smell of the open tubs of honey maddened their senses. They began as stippled black lines, then the lines grew heavier, thicker, twisted on the wall like eels, their tails evasive, their heads spreading out and disappearing. Where? Into the open jaws of the traps, of course. Like twisted roots they emerge and rise from the walls.

I don't know how much time passed as I looked on. I don't know how long I had slept, how often I woke up in the dark with my ears full of groaning.

I don't know how often I met my wife's eyes.

I must have gone down to the grocer's on the corner, in my slippers, to buy more jars of "Choice Honey." I kicked the neighbor's dog who got under my feet; he looked a rather pitiable sight to me for all his proud barking. My wife Rachel sipped honey from a glass, that much I'm sure of; she crooked her tongue like a spoon. I'm sure I must also have eaten something of what Bilha had left on our roof, but I don't remember what. I dreamed that a very wide tongue, like a boxer's, slid over my face, and I was melting away with pleasure and was sure it was my wife Rachel.

Suddenly it was morning, I can't say of which day, but with it came a great silence. The light was dim like that of a neon lamp. My wife sat on her side, her arm on the bed, her head on her arm, and her hair all around. The flesh of her bare arm was as white as alabaster.

The jars were black with ants. Their corpses lay in the surrounding water, too. The room looked like a battlefield after the battle. The ceiling was smooth, like a dead man's forehead; in the walls there were cracks like gaping lips, furrows like cuts in flesh, breaches like rows of rotten teeth—but clean, clean of ants. Suddenly the scars in the wall looked to me like signs of strength. Now I believed in the strength of our building. I had saved the house, I had routed the enemy.

I approached Rachel with tears of victory in my eyes. I laid my hand on her bare shoulder. Her shoulder was cold—I let my hand slide over her hair, I raised it and stroked her neck. The skin of her neck was soft and smooth and solid and elastic all at once—but cold.

I looked at my wife Rachel's head and thought about the proper way to announce my victory to her. Her smooth long hair with its coppery shine lay loose around her head like a diadem. When the business of the traps had started and we had sat hunched up looking at what was going on, her hair had been gathered on the back of her head; now it was loose. I remembered that I had seen her dancing naked between the jars of honey without stumbling over them, her loose hair fluttering like a wing around her head, on fire whenever it caught a ray of light.

I insisted on plaiting her hair into a kind of wreath around her head. My hesitating hands (ever since I had come to her bed by force, the skin of her body shrank at the touch of my hand and I didn't dare touch her) trembled, and to distract myself I thought of the wreathed head of the Roman soldier on the calendar.

"A golden ribbon for your hair," I said soundlessly, "a charm."

"No," I heard her voice from between her locks of hair.

Her voice was tired and self-indulgent—and peculiar.

I grunted something that might be taken as a question.

"You're getting me dirty."

"I'll wash my hands."

"I want honey. I'm thirsty."

"There's no more honey and no more—ants."

"You sure?"

"Yes." I tried to make her feel all of the weight of victory in that monosyllable. I tried to tell her: I am the victor, but the wreath of victory I wind around your head.

"No," Rachel said in the same tired, self-indulgent, strange tone, and her fingers unraveled what I'd already finished plaiting.

"Why not?"

"You're making me dirty."

I went to wash my hands.

When I came back with a glass of water in my hands, Rachel was lying on her back, laughing a lazy spoiled laugh. I held out the glass to her but Rachel looked neither at me nor at the glass: her feet, covered to the ankles by a nightgown white as a wedding dress, were drumming on the bed like they do when I tickled their soles. And I had not tickled the soles of her feet for many days now. Not since before that night when I had come to her bed by force.

How charming Rachel was then, with her playfulness, her laughter, and her joyful drumming feet. My heart ached, the glass trembled in my hand, and I didn't know what to do. I went down on my knees and tried to kiss the soles of her feet.

My wife's laughter turned to silence. She withdrew her feet from me, withdrew them and enfolded them within her gown, and her pure white gown danced where her feet had been kicking in excitement. What had excited her feet?

"Ants." I heard my own frightened answer, and I looked around.

The honey jars were again crawling with life. Bridges of live ants spanned the moats, a raft of live ants holding each other by means of their mandibles. And black, very quick ants, the likes of which I had not yet seen in our house, were galloping across. They crossed and without wasting a minute, climbed up into the honey jars, dashed over the layers of the drowned, collected as much honey as they could manage and disappeared back by way of the living bridge of ants that hung across the water.

"Very powerful ants," I said to myself. "Nothing stops them, not even the honey, not even the honey."

I caught one ant—with difficulty—and while I was biting back the pain of its sting, I studied its head through the magnifying glass. It was clear from the head and the appendages that we were dealing with a new, very powerful race. The head flowed toward the mandibles in perfect conical shape. It seemed as though a great, invisible force was being compressed into that narrow place. At that point the snout split into two limbs, pointed and bent like horns. One sees immediately that each of those pointed limbs may serve its owner as a saw, or as a file, by the use of the perforated and ridged skin on its back. The edge of the limbs, the curve of their edge, and their pliability—they can be turned ninety degrees in each direction—indicate their many possible uses. As levering tools, as drilling tools, as penetrating tools, as hollow needles for injecting venom—I had felt their sting in the flesh of my finger—and also as sucking tools, depending on the circumstances. Add to that the use of both horns as a forklift, or, when turned to face each other, as a pair of pincers. I could even envisage their conical, flexible head being used in wartime to swing the pair of horns like a crushing two-edged sword. I called it the bronze ant.

"And it can even resist the temptation of the honey," I said to my dismayed self.

Chapter VI

The ants treat me with disdain—
I plug breaches and raise retaining walls.

The naïve, weak, and even somewhat submissive laxity with which Rachel was lying, nude and white, in the sun on the roof, only increased my feeling, of debasement. I knew I needed to act, I needed to mend the wound with deeds.

"Be a man," I silently encouraged myself.

But what turned my determination into warlike wrath was the seemingly harmless fact that this new race of ants had no interest in concealing its intentions in the least. They destroyed openly, rushing here and there in plain sight, disregarding all the rules of camouflage. That I could not tolerate. Theirs was just an indifferent, careless disdain—amusing, I would have said, if I hadn't been on the receiving end of the joke. As it happened, a thin nylon handkerchief—Rachel's—was dragged inside a wall; I just managed to see its tail slipping in and disappearing.

"Be a man," I told myself, and went to work.

I planned two parallel lines of defense. One tactical: stopping up the cracks in the wall as soon as they appeared. The other, a long-term strategic project: brick walls on the inside of the drywall. That way, if the ants should manage to ruin the interior walls—the ones that divided the kitchen from the room and the one between the main room and the hall—which contained part of the building's concrete skeleton, these other walls would stand ready to take over the full weight of the ceiling.

I had no illusions about my new walls, my supporting walls, that their fate would be any different than the first, but meanwhile, during the time the ants would need to gnaw through the second walls, I would build a third set and so on—and between building one wall and the other I would, for all the murderous industry of those ants, find a little time to rest and recover my strength.

I am a builder. The materials I needed were neither many nor expensive. White plaster, white cement, broken concrete bricks, fired bricks, ordinary cement, a pail, a level, and trowels. I stacked them all properly, in an attempt to maintain a minimum of order and cleanliness among the fine dust that sifted incessantly from the cracks, splits, and breaches that multiplied continually. First I intended to stack the materials on the roof, but I soon realized that in order to keep up with the murderous pace of the ants, I would have to stay in the room all the time, with my eyes on the wall and my hands on my tools. Even so, I had very little time left for building the retaining walls. I tried to gain time by disregarding the narrow cracks—like shallow scratches, not too dangerous really—that must have been caused by the movement in the wall. I filled only the wide gaps, those the size of a hand or larger, by pushing pieces of brick into them and sealing them over with a mixture of plaster and cement. I had learned that strengthening the plaster with cement could fortify the wall for as much as a whole day before being broken down again by the angry ants.

These little tricks of the trade, and also my skilled builder's hands, won me short pauses in which I could wash my hands and face, eat something, and take a nap.

Deep in her heart, my wife Rachel must have respected my work. She didn't interrupt me with talk, complaints, or demands. She kept Bilha out of the room completely, and amused herself with her friend on the rush mat on the roof. I could tell from the way they held back their laughter. We stopped eating cooked food or setting the table. There was just no time. At irregular intervals I would grab a sandwich or two that my wife Rachel would send in to me with Bilha. The rest of the time I ate olives. My pockets were full of them. Rachel and Bilha would drag out their wailing laughter like cars, but when they would pass through the room, they would walk on tiptoe and keep silent, Bilha with a handkerchief pressed to her lips. Rachel her lips open and her eyes attentive.

Once my wife asked me:

"How is the new house coming?"

I didn't know whether she was asking in earnest. She was eating honey. And when my wife Rachel eats honey, who knows what goes on in her mind. I told her that I wouldn't entrust the building of our house to others for long. I told her that as soon as I had repelled the ant invasion, I would work day and night on our new house. I swore to her that she should never doubt it, and as she stuck out her tongue full length to lick the saucer, I couldn't tell whether her eyes were gleaming with the taste of honey or with a vision of our new house.

I told her that the date for finishing the house was written on the calendar, and we must on no account be late. Rachel moved her tongue against her cheek and said lackadaisically, "Good," and again I didn't know what she really meant.

Chapter VII

*My wife admires the ants—She decorates the cracks and splits
and makes them look like dragons—I suspect my wife Rachel of
maintaining secret communications with the ants—
My wife Rachel brings me to my knees.*

Once I saw my wife Rachel standing at the wall that divides the
main room from the kitchen—the first that I expected would give
me trouble—with the palms of her hands on her breasts and her
eyes staring at a line of ants.

"Isn't it wonderful!" That's what she said.

A line of ants were coming out of the crack and attacking the
wall from the outside—a new technique. One might explain it as
follows: while this line of ants was attacking the wall from the one
side, a corresponding line of ants was chewing the wall up from
the other—a pincer movement, coordinated from inside the room,
with jaws closing in on the wall from both sides. Apparently, we
had just witnessed the debut of an innovative and highly dangerous
ant tactic.

"Wonderful," Rachel whispered, enchanted.

"What's wonderful about it?" I thundered. "They're ruining our
home."

"Yes," Rachel said very quietly.

"Disgusting saboteurs," I hissed.

"Disgusting saboteurs," Rachel repeated after me, and then added with the same strange calm, her voice as enchanted as her eyes: "Wonderful."

Their insolence cost them dearly. I crushed them against the wall by the score, I trod dozens underfoot, and the few that ran off I caught and cracked like lice. A couple of hours later, when the wall cracked in exactly the same spot on the inside of the main room, accompanied by a dull rolling sound, not a single ant was to be found in the opening.

Was this a reprisal?

At any rate, Rachel sat on the bed, her eyes on the crack in the wall. Then something like a smile flitted over her thin lips—and she took to decorating the apartment.

What decorating means in a building where the walls are cracked and crumbling and fine dust sifts down from them all over the place is hard to say. Perhaps we had better call it *rearranging* the house— an attempt to make it look suitable for its new state of being, the reality of the ants.

She wore a long dressing gown, a kind of kimono covered with trees and little streams, ancient castles, rocks, and dragons. The breaches I stop up, she covers; the cracks I ignore, she decorates; and there are many of those little cracks. They crowd around the breaches by the score, like the furrowy wrinkles around an old man's eyes. A few strokes of lipstick alternating with eyebrow pencil are enough to make a network of wrinkly cracks look like a castle with a sloping roof at the head of a promontory, with scaly dragons posted like sentries at its entrance. The entrance, naturally, being the opening of a breach in the wall—the dangerous worsening of the crack I was now in such a hurry to stop up.

There were, of course, also isolated cracks, and if they were linked with the other cracks according to some plan, I knew nothing about it. These Rachel would camouflage. She covered them with pictures or with colored ribbons. The pictures from the large calendar in the kitchen, the Coliseum, the Arch of Titus, the antiquities of Pompeii, a couple of Jupiters and Etna belching orange smoke—it was an Italian calendar—the wonders of the ancient world covered the cracks. Then an ant nimbly cut away Titus's Arch and disappeared with it inside the crack.

I followed her fingers at work—they moved, twisted like transparent pink eels. I neglected my own work and observed hers, and in doing so I discovered something that, I thought, would have a far-reaching effect on our war strategy.

I saw Rachel putting up a picture in a place where there was no crack, and I asked her why.

"You sure there's no crack?" Rachel asked.

The words were still on her lips when there was a cracking sound, and fine, sandy dust was sifting down from the new opening.

Now I understood—something that somehow neither surprised nor annoyed me, though in other circumstances it would have made me see red and suspect my wife of treason: Rachel was not only able to hear the sound of the gnawing inside the walls but could also guess its location and direction. A kind of mysterious radar. I had to cast off suspicion and fear and set my mind to exploiting this ability.

But my eyes were full of lust and my hands lay still. The mortar was dry on my trowel and I could not turn away from the enchanting movements of Rachel's body at work. Her dressing gown was tied with a blue sash whose ends danced as she moved. Her knees, white buds, swung alternately between the parting of her dressing gown, her heels went up-and-down, up-and-down, alive, sentient, graceful, as if they, not her hands, were doing the work.

To say that I felt something seething up in me does not capture the sensation. Something seething to burst out, like a jet of venom. What could I do?

One leap, and like a suicide, with the trowel toy like in my hand, I buried my head in Rachel's belly, almost to the neck, waiting for the humiliation that was to come, that had to come.

"On your knees," Rachel commanded.

I knelt, head lowered, eyes closed. Then Rachel laid her hand on my forehead, and I opened my eyes. I saw her murmuring something, her eyes staring into space.

I didn't know what her lips were murmuring. I didn't know whether it was a blessing or a curse, and I didn't know what connection there was between this murmuring and the humming that rose then from inside the walls, rose and died down. Her hand on my forehead was a gift of grace, more than I could contain.

For a while, even after she had taken her hand from my forehead, I was deprived of all power to fight. I admonished myself, gave a long speech, the long and the short of which was: no time to wallow in emotion, time for war, be a man! Fully conscious of my duty, I wanted to jump to my feet, but I was unable. For a long while I went on arguing with my legs, until at last they straightened out and I rose from the ground.

Chapter VIII

In my imagination, my wife Rachel looks both like a daughter of Israel and a Roman Legionary—I study the ways and tactics of the ants—What form my wife Rachel's help takes—My ration of sleep is cut—Bilha pulls me to the floor—My wife Rachel and I reject Bilha's offer for us to go and live with her temporarily to escape the danger of our building falling down—First hint of understanding between my wife Rachel and me.

It is a miracle how often my wife Rachel crosses my path within the four square yards of our apartment without seeing me. I'm not exactly elastic, but even when there's only a hand's width between me and the doorpost, my wife Rachel now gets by without touching me. And her look is like that, too: she floats and glides and does not see, like light.

Perhaps Rachel doesn't see me, but I can't take my eyes off her. When she stops decorating the walls, she puts on a white smock, like a nurse's, and goes out into the sun. The smock is bright white, but the neck that buds from it is whiter, almost bluish with whiteness. Strange that the fine dust that drifts down incessantly doesn't turn her smock gray. Even the ants, which are everywhere in our house, do not climb on her white smock. But then they dwell in her bosom, or so I suspect whenever I see the apples of her breasts dancing inside the lapels of her white smock, her lower lip turning down and her hand spread out like a sentry at the gateway to her breasts.

When she doesn't wear the kimono for decorating or the white smock for other activities, Rachel wraps herself in a sheet. As she comes out of the shower on her way to the roof, naked and dripping, she is trailed by an escort of thirsty ants. When she comes back from the roof, from the sun, wrapped in a sheet with a white scarf on her head, half the sheet trails behind her like a royal train. Her walk is a dance, her posture proud, noble, and virginal. Where have I seen this before?

In my imagination, with the aid of the large calendar in our kitchen, I see my wife doubled. Wearing a white gown and presented in profile, from one side of a fortress on a rock or what remains of it, there gazes a Daughter of Israel, one of those who goes out to the vineyards to be abducted—what else? People don't go out there for the sand. But why hasn't she been abducted? Because no one dares to crumple or stain her pure, smooth virgin's gown—so that she may continue going to the vineyards to be abducted, and so forth. And a young man in a toga stands there too, a boy almost, and I swear that Rachel looks like him as well, like that Roman boy, clean-faced, clear-faced, a boy forever, perhaps because time has worn away his eyes, and in the picture, presented in profile, he, wearing a toga, faces the Daughter of Israel dressed in white, with two hollows for eyes, clean and clear-skinned, and also merry. And I imagine Rachel as a Roman boy in a white virgin's gown dancing between the ruins of the rock, terraces, stones, cracked walls, headless columns, relics of decoration, all in cheerful colors.

"Careful," my wife said in a worried tone, and she removed a curious bronze ant that had been wandering over the ruins on the rock in the calendar. She put it on the drainboard. Proud, cold, practical, the ant immediately turned to the nearest opening in the wall. The ant says nothing, but there is no better preacher, says the proverb. I took the ant's example and went back to my work.

The trouble is, the rate at which the bronze ants spread is so fast that sometimes I can't quite take it. Of course, there are entire parts of the apartment that the ants, as far as one can see from outside the walls in any case, have not yet touched. The center wall (between the main room and the hall), the frame of the long window, the part of the floor with the bed, the entire ceiling, and the corners where the ceiling meets the walls—and anyone who knows anything about building knows that while all of these walls are sound, there's no real danger of a collapse. On the other hand, if you want to bring the whole house down, there's no need to chew up the ceiling: you need only destroy its supports. Actually, the thicker and more solid the ceiling, the more likely it is to kill you if it falls—and you have to give this old house credit for one thing at least: the people who built it ignored the engineers' specifications; believing as they did that houses should last forever, they spared no expense in providing excellent materials. So the ceilings in this house are very heavy and very sound—woe to us all should they ever come down.

No need to panic, as yet, I think. If I gather together all those little lumps of fine, yellowish dirt the ants have raked out from under the tiles and inside the walls, I doubt whether it would fill even a single bucket. I know, of course, that the real danger is within the walls themselves. They grind and gnaw from the inside. But, as I've said, there is no immediate danger. First, I check two or three times a day, knocking with a finger knuckle on every place on the wall that seems suspect and marking the places that sound hollow. This allows me to follow the process of the ants inside the wall and to calculate their pace.

My wife was angry about the crooked marks I'd made on the wall with a thick carpenter's pencil, but to my great surprise, she didn't ask me to erase them. On the contrary, she laughed a great deal in her quiet, muffled way, and took an interest in every line I added. And when there came to be a lot of them, my wife added a line here and a line there until we found ourselves collaborating on all kinds of ceremonial shapes, candelabra, ram's horns, lions, and snakes that looked like illuminations, their eyes without guile and their mouths gaping from the breaches in the wall. Rachel found this all quite harmless and entertaining.

Second, I hear them at their manifold operations within the walls. I have learned to distinguish the different sounds: the scratching of the scrapers, whose job is grinding down the hard edges; the clinking of the drillers, who use their sharp mandibles to burrow in from the outside and out from the inside; the pounding of the hammerheads, who were the first to open the breaches and whose work is sometimes accompanied by dull plopping sounds; the sawing of the saw-edge bearers, whose work produces the humming background tune that contains all the other sounds. This one you have to be particularly careful of, because of its relaxing, soporific quality. Still, it was only at times of deep silence outside and great awareness inside that I could distinguish between the different components of this giant army at work. Unfortunately, those times were rare.

I also had to allow for the possibility that its true vanguard might be camouflaged by shrewd diverting and misleading devices, such as silencers, the use of frequencies the human ear cannot perceive, and then maliciously exaggerated noises in one place, usually in the center of the apartment, to cover advances on the flank. Against that there was no easy defense. Only alertness, alertness. I reduced my ration of sleep to a couple of hours a day. And I tried—yes—to enlist my wife's keen hearing for my campaign.

My wife has slightly protruding, funnel-shaped ears—perhaps the only flaw in the harmony of her features. But it seems to have given her a very fine sense of hearing. When the ant invasion intensified, Rachel put another two hairpins at the sides of her head and so kept her ears unobstructed. And yet, I still do not know whether it was her ears that did the hearing, or her raised eyebrows, or her slightly open mouth, or the quivering of her nostrils, or her legs that would suddenly freeze as the olive tint of her eyes lightened and her hands gathered in her lap as if propelled by a hidden force. The first time I saw her like that I was alarmed and called out in a voice that sounded strange even to myself:

"What do you hear, Rachel?"

But Rachel didn't react; not a muscle moved in her radiant face. No doubt about it: Rachel was hearing something I couldn't hear. This reassured me: one more vile tactic they could not use. But it also made me feel vulnerable. What was she hearing? Why did she glow all over just because of some sound or sounds I was entirely incapable of hearing? Did she feel some sort of affinity with the sources of those sounds? Were not my enemies my wife's enemies as well?

It was easy enough to suspect my wife, but what good did it do? If my wife had betrayed me and was in league with my enemies, then all that was left to me was to huddle up in a corner and wait for the collapse. When a man is in trouble, he interprets everything as working in his favor—and is saved.

So when I discovered the imprint of my wife's tongue in the remains of honey confection that contained ant corpses by the score, I told myself that Rachel's tongue had been at the candy before the ants had arrived; and if someone were to say that my own eyes had seen the candy crawling with ants before Rachel had touched it, still it was possible that both Rachel and the ants had eaten from the same piece of candy without their touching her or her touching them. And even if Rachel had eaten the candy with the ants already on it, surely she had not done so from love—one doesn't eat one's ally. In short, I talked myself into calming down. Still, I wasn't completely at ease until I laid out the cadaver of an ant on the drainboard and examined it.

It was lying on its back now, arched toward its legs. Its legs, antennae, and mandibles all pointed toward each other, as though inspecting one another; were they of any use? When the answer was no, they died, apparently so as not to be a burden to the others and hold up their work.

I was studying the antennae of this bold ant—unfortunately, I had not yet been able to examine one of them alive, so fast, clever and maneuverable were they—when I felt the thick, moist breath of our neighbor Bilha on my face. I don't know what Bilha was looking at, but her face was very close to mine, and I believe that the other parts of her body were not too far distant either. Let us leave her for a moment in that embarrassing situation, and before we allow her to whisper two hard words in my ear, let us say a few things about her.

Bilha wears widow's weeds. Years ago, they say, she was married to her half-stepbrother and they weren't allowed to have any children, in case they should turn out to be monsters. She was very beautiful, and her stepbrother, that is to say, her husband, imagined that she was cheating on him all the time and often beat her. Strangely enough, the beatings didn't spoil her looks and even made her eyes and such appear more alluring. Finally, her brother-husband accused her of having an affair with some old, lonely bachelor who was living nearby. Then he tied a rope to a hook in the ceiling and hanged himself.

The story of her affair with the old man was absolutely true. Bilha loved to help people. That was her greatest passion—perhaps her only one. Her widow's weeds were very becoming. She was a little chubby but not like those fat women whose bodies spread every which way when they walk. Her flesh was firm, only her curves curved more, so that draped in black—all her dresses were black—they looked like restrained impulses, and that made her attractive to many men. But Bilha only went where she could help. Where a wife was barren and the husband demanded a child, Bilha would turn up and become pregnant, give birth, and then depart. Her babies were good-looking and healthy, and both parties were better off for it. Bilha was paid well—though she never asked for anything, since she regarded her help as a good work that brought its own reward—and with that the babies were no longer hers. Even now there was no black widow's gown, tight or loose, of which Bilha did not look about to burst free. When Bilha walks, you always hear at least a couple of pairs of shoes. If I hadn't heard the patter of two or three pairs of shoes that day, it was because she had taken them off, and there she was beside me, barefoot. All I saw was her left eyebrow, so close was her pleasant face to mine. But the eyebrow was ugly, drawn in with a fat black crayon, and below it were a couple of hairs that remained from her natural brow.

"Your wife is barren," Bilha said to me. As if I didn't know. My wife would never tolerate a foreign body inside of her. She would expel it and add a parting gift—retchings of disgust. That was how it had been on our wedding night, and that was how it had been on the Sabbath when I had taken her by force. For hours she had washed herself in the shower. Her wedding nightgown hung in the wardrobe with a stain of shame on its seam. She never wore that nightgown, but neither did she throw it away. For years it had been hanging in the closet. We hadn't even told the rabbi these little details. Only we two knew them. At least, that was what I thought until now.

"Mrs. Gal," I whispered angrily, "Why are you saying such things about my wife?"

"I am not Mrs. Gal," Bilha said in that same dull voice of hers that sounded as if it was being squeezed out of her flesh. "I am Rachel's friend."

"And are you my friend, too?" I asked to annoy her.

"If you like, if you like," she said.

"You're Mrs. Gal, that's what you are," I said and felt my knees weaken.

"I'm Bilha, I'm Bilha," she whispered. "I only want to help."

"If you're not Mrs. Gal, then you're just an old maid. There, that's what you are. You're just an old maid."

"A widow, if you please."

"All right, an old widow."

"Not old—experienced. If you please. Experienced."

Her big chest nearly muzzled me, and her voice was a kind of panting, accompanied by whispered laughs, such as I had only heard when she and my wife were at their little games. And I couldn't bear it. Though I kept silent. The years had taught me to suffer in silence. I kept silent, but my bowels churned inside me: any foreign body between my wife and myself was hateful to me. Inside me, in my mind, I always spilled their blood out of jealousy. Surely it was this that had made me rise to wage war so uncompromisingly against the black ant?

"An old maid," I insisted. "Yes, an old maid and not Mrs. Gal and not an experienced widow. And if you don't like it, there's the door, Mrs. Gal." I wanted to point at the door, but the floor was in my way.

"You want me to go?" she asked straight out of her chest and into my mouth. "But it's not me who's holding you, but the other way around."

It is true that the two of us were tangled up on the floor like a ball of string—and yet I felt sure that she was lying, of course, shamelessly. The floor of our kitchen is all of a yard and a half long and half a yard wide, and all she needed was to play her shabby little game of pretending to lose her balance and cling to my shoulders that were then bending over the ant and drag me after her onto the floor. Easy to fall, but hard to get up. And there she was, all groans and panting laughter, and me—nothing but rage.

"Rachela, Rachela," Bilha called from the floor, "come and listen to something nice."

As I got to my feet, shaking the dust from my trousers—a silly thing to do, since there was no longer any place in our house free from that dust—and trying to get my breathing under control, I saw Rachel's lovely head rising slowly from behind the doorway to the hall, her eyes shining and curious. Bilha smoothed out her dress and gave Rachel a shy laugh, as if to say: "I tried, but . . ."

"There, that's what you are," I shouted, a sudden attack of nerves and tore the brooch—an enamel beetle—from Bilha's chest, as though at a court martial, and threw it at Rachel's feet.

Bilha wanted to cry but laughed. Then she covered her chest with her hands, as though ashamed of those breasts that had been of no avail, and hurried out of the apartment.

Not an hour had passed before Bilha returned, her face made up, wearing another black dress, holding a bottle of wine and a Pyrex bowl full of all kinds of food. My appetite had been diminishing lately, as my sense of danger had grown more acute. I would willingly have done without the chicken and the mashed potatoes and the pickles and the cold white wine on that terribly hot day, so as not to stop the work of shoring the building up.

But, as the food was there, and Rachel was eating, and the table was laid, I also sat down to dinner.

First, however, Bilha offered to have us over to her place. We refused this offer. Then she proposed that we eat on the roof. I said that I didn't object to Rachel and Bilha eating on the roof, but that I had to stay inside—and actually I was surprised that Mrs. Gal didn't understand on her own that it would be pure madness to leave the inside of the house and abandon it to the ants.

We ate in silence, listening for any sign of the ants. Our table wasn't set in the usual sense. It was covered with brown-white dust, like everything else in the house. But since we regarded that merely as a temporary inconvenience, we didn't go to any trouble, and since we used no knives and forks, only our hands, we could also do without the rest of the tableware, napkins and all that. Rachel and I sat facing each other on stools on either side of the table, and Bilha sat on our bed. Even though she was sitting opposite me,

Rachel didn't look at me; her eyes were always elsewhere. She sat straight, proud, still, her nostrils widening a little as she put some chicken into her mouth, but for all that she finished her portion well before we finished ours. She sat without moving and listened. Then her eyes began to sparkle. I could not say from where in the wall it came, that dull roll of thunder that almost congealed my blood. When my wife's eyes sparkle, the olive-green turns lighter and floods her pupils and leaves nothing of them but two fading vertical lines. Bilha was frightened, her eyes jumped from Rachel to me and from me to Rachel; she shook a single ant from the heights of her bosom and cried:

"The walls are coming down!"

"Yes, yes," Rachel said, wonderfully calm.

"The house is crawling with ants . . . crawling . . . crawling . . ." Bilha said, and disgustedly shook a few more of them off her widow's gown.

"Oh yes," said Rachel proudly. "They get everywhere, everywhere."

"We're moving to another house soon," I said, and thought, what business do they have in the pleats of Bilha's dress?

"When?" Bilha asked. I told her the date. Rachel listened indifferently, her glance hanging on Bilha's fingers shaking ants from the pleats of her dress.

"But," Bilha objected, "Who knows what might happen . . . even . . ." she slapped her hand over her mouth so as not to say what might happen. Confused, she rose and went to Rachel and fell on her knees before her:

"Rachela, Rachela, I'm worried. Come to my place, both of you. I have two empty rooms. They are at your disposal. Stay with me until your new house is finished, I beg you . . ." She embraced Rachel's legs—a plague on her!—as I had wanted to do so often and had never managed. Bilha's hands were bare, and Rachel's legs were also bare under her white smock, and Bilha's bare, fleshy hands twisted around Rachel's bare legs—four limbs, like twisting adders.

Yet, wonder of wonders—Rachel did not spare her a glance. She looked at me. At first there was greenish bright ice in her eyes, that armored look in which she entrenched herself whenever I—her lawful wedded husband—tried to touch her. Now Rachel's legs were frozen, numb at last to the touch of Bilha's imploring hands.

"Only to help," Bilha moaned between tears. "Me, I only want to help . . ." She was desperate, hysterical. She wanted to demonstrate her readiness to help and for lack of anything else caught a coal-black ant on Rachel's white thigh—poor woman. Immediately she gave out a shriek, took her hands off Rachel's legs, and put her bitten, burning finger, throbbing with venom, into her mouth, moaning partly from pain, partly from worry.

"Impossible," Rachel said in a whisper. "Impossible," I said too, at the same moment, soundlessly, whisper for whisper, syllable for syllable together with Rachel, I looked at Rachel and Rachel looked at me. We had never looked at each other that way, Rachel and I. It seems that we even smiled the same smile. How to otherwise explain the fact that Bilha now looked at me and Rachel alternately, with an expression of astonishment and fear, and could find no words as she rose, the sting forgotten in her mouth, and withdrew from the room, walking backward?

"Look," Rachel called to me while she squatted down and held out her open hand, and on it a bronze ant, a horse of an ant, one of those that I had just now examined under the magnifying glass.

Rachel was a real genius when it came to the miniature, microscopic, delicate. What I discovered under the magnifying glass, Rachel had discovered with her ears, her nostrils, or perhaps with some sense I could not imagine. She brought her hands to mine, and the ant rapidly crossed over to my hand and climbed my forearm. I touched my forearm to hers, and the ant crossed to her forearm and climbed to her upper arm. Her upper arm touched mine, and suddenly we found ourselves arm in arm and Rachel looked at me, not with desire, but not with repulsion either, with something new that I find very hard to define or even to comprehend—but my heart grew larger within me.

At any rate I felt clearly that Rachel and I now shared a secret.

Chapter IX

A visit from my assistant that ends badly—
I lose the ledger and Bilha.

The very next day Bilha returned to us, a bandage on her sore finger, and a combination of compassion and reproof in her eyes. She did not come alone. With her came the assistant foreman of my work crew, Moshe Kattan, a big fellow with steady hands and a slow mind, wholly dedicated to his work. Which was the reason I had made him my assistant. What Bilha wanted from Moshe, or what Moshe, who is married to a dumpy, irritable wife, wanted from Bilha, I did not know. Perhaps they had just met by chance in front of our door. At any rate, they came without hesitation: Bilha ran to Rachel, and Moshe bared his strong teeth to me.

I stood there, awkward. I didn't know whether his teeth were exposed in a threatening grin or in a friendly smile. I wanted to be polite and friendly but couldn't remember why or for what reason I should bother. Certainly, this man who had been working with me for years deserved a clap on the shoulder: unfortunately, I could not clap him on the shoulder without soiling his white shirt—he must have put it on specially for this visit—with my mortar-covered hands.

Moshe looked at me and looked at the room and blinked and wiped his forehead with the back of his arm, then let his eyes rest on me and said:

"So what about it?"

A new hole had opened up in the wall and I had been about to stop it up with brick and mortar as he had come in. The wall was gaping, and there he was standing and waiting for an explanation, and I hadn't even offered him a chair. I wanted to put it all right, but Moshe was standing there, feet apart, as though planting himself, with his lips curving down slightly—just like when he saw me putting up a scaffolding with split planks and wanted to draw my attention to it without embarrassing me in front of the whole crew.

"Sit down, sit down," I said to him, "an important guest like you," but with my exaggerated politeness I only complicated the situation, for there was nowhere to sit down. On the bed, the only thing still standing apart from the heaps of bricks, sand, and mortar, there wasn't a hand's breadth free of Rachel's sheets, smock, and all that—for while Rachel had been as careful as ever about keeping her body clean and decorating the walls, now she had begun to be a little careless about her clothes, which she used less and less and which she shed with the indifference of a reptile shedding its old skin.

Moshe sat down on the bed, sank into a heap of woman's things, and fixed his eyes on me severely.

"We've been worried about you," he said finally. "The contractor says, what do I care, Jacob or no Jacob, the job has to get done, and on time." So I ran to the kitchen to the calendar, leafed through it hurriedly, and called out:

"There's the date, you see, it's written down here."

"So what if it's written down?"

"So it's written down, there."

"I said," Moshe insisted, "What's the good if it's written down?"

"Of course it's written down. It would hardly be a good idea not to have it written down?"

"I didn't say that . . ."

"You'd better pay attention to what you've said and what you haven't, Moshe Kattan."

I wanted to put him in his place, or, actually, I just wanted him to go away and leave me alone. There was more than enough to do here without any contractors' errand boys.

"All right," Moshe said after he had thought it over for a while. "So how much time do we have left?"

"How much time? I'll tell you in a minute." Again I ran to the calendar in the kitchen and leafed through it hurriedly. But I couldn't remember whether I had torn off last week's page. And Rachel, how many had Rachel torn to use in decorating the walls? Could I help it that the pace of the creatures in the walls didn't keep time with the calendar in the kitchen?

And how could I know how many days and nights had passed since the ants had started their invasion and how many were still left? I did not know what to tell Moshe. But it was he who helped me out:

"There! You see? Only a couple of weeks."

"A couple of weeks, sure," I said.

"But how do you think anything will get done if everybody is busy with his own house? The contractor says he's been sending you notes and you haven't even taken the trouble to reply."

"Maybe." I made an effort to remember. Moshe's look encouraged me to do so; there was a somewhat friendly shrewdness in it. "Yes. I've even kept them in the ledger. Everything is there."

"Thank God, thank God." Moshe stood up and shook out his pants. Then he stretched and yawned, and his hand flew up to his mouth and raked a single black ant from the corner of his lips. I saw its perfect antennae beat uselessly in the air—an embarrassing situation for an ant—but its jaws were still stuck in the thick skin of Moshe the builder.

"Just a moment," I shouted and snatched the ant from his fingers and laid it on a little heap of sand.

Moshe burst out with a big laugh, grabbed my hand, and gave it a strong shake. "I told the contractor, as long as Jacob is alive, I will be his assistant. And now, I told him, now that Jacob isn't here, I will take his place."

"Thank you, thank you," I said. I drawled out the words, so that even a deaf man couldn't have missed the irony of my gratitude. I had known since he arrived that Moshe had come only to see which way the wind was blowing. I laughed to myself and made my voice sound carefree:

"I'm no longer foreman. You're the foreman now."

My guest tried to smile and be angry at the same time, but the two attempts collided and deprived him of his speech. He had walked into the trap I had set for him. If he rejected my statement, he would commit himself, to eternal servitude, so to speak, to his master— namely, me. If he accepted it, he would be admitting my right to appoint him foreman in my place. For a while he stood silent, then he hesitated, and then he said in a whisper:

"We thought you were reliable."

"Yes," I answered. My mind was on the exterior wall of the room, which was swelling, right under my eyes, near the window frame.

"I've never heard of a foreman leaving his crew in the middle of a job, not for all the money in the world. We thought you were reliable."

"Listen, mister," I couldn't hold myself back any longer, "you're talking to me about reliability? Who has kept our accounts to the last decimal? Who has guarded our ledger like his own child? Reliable, you say, but who, if you please, Assistant Foreman Kattan, has used that word more often than I? Perhaps you remember, Mister Kattan—if your memory hasn't become too confused by some base, indecent ambition, of course—perhaps you remember what is written on the little brass souvenir I gave you when I made you my assistant? Reliability. And why reliability? Because with reliability you build a house, and without reliability you destroy it. That's it. You destroy it. Hhh!"—a snort of pleasure escaped from within me—"here they come. Do you hear them? First with a whispering, creeping, rubbing sound, a few grains dropping, a casual gnawing, then a continuous chewing noise with sounds of grinding and drilling in it, and *crrrack*—the first blast, and then a disturbing hum, day and night, then millions of little grains shifting from place to place to make room for trillions of little grains shifting from place to place to make room . . ."

Rachel, from the roof, from the sun, stopped the flow of my words with a gesture of her hand—both of us, Moshe and I, had been advancing step by step, face to face, with me pushing him back all the time, till we reached the door to the roof—while her other hand held the sheet that barely covered her breasts and belly.

"Mr. Kattan wants to say something," Bilha's voice rose from behind the sheet—she must have been naked, too, abandoned to the sun, tanning. Moshe didn't even look at them, his face was glued to mine and he repeated as though for the tenth time, enunciating precisely but in an incongruous whisper:

"Give me the ledger."

"A man should defend his house," I cried and looked at Rachel over Moshe's shoulder. I looked angrily, reprovingly, but didn't know how to reprimand her without making Moshe turn around. "And that too is being reliable."

"Give me the ledger," Moshe repeated.

"As you wish." I told him, adopting a somewhat formal tone. "The ledger is a very important book. Everything is written down in it, Mr. Kattan, and you can tell the contractor, whatever his name is, Kerzenbaum, the same thing. There is nothing missing there, I've put every spare hour of my life into keeping it. I keep it right next to that other Book in fact, Mr. Kattan. It has its place of honor on the bookshelf . . ."

But it was not on the bookshelf. The Book was lying there, in its usual place—covered by a thin layer of dust that had sifted down from the walls—but the ledger was gone. I tried to remember where I had left it. When had I last held the ledger? What had I done with the ledger? Not, of course, that I let Moshe notice my confusion. On the contrary, I was still telling him, here, here is the ledger, in a minute you'll get the ledger, just a moment, just a moment. I walked up and down the room with my eyes on the floor. The room wasn't large and there was really nowhere to look. But I kept searching so as not to meet Moshe's eyes. I pushed my head under the bed, finding a major column of ants, and made a mental note of it. But I did not see the ledger there. I looked for it under the armchair, under the easy chair, under the night table. Suddenly I remembered, and crawled to the tile skirting around the kitchen floor. There—I recalled—I had used it as a footstool while plugging a particularly high crack—on the wall. First I came across my bookmark. I sniffed at the bookmark, and guided by its smell I started to dig with both hands—as I had seen the ants do—in a little heap of sand mixed with mortar. I had prepared this little heap in the middle of the room so that I could use it to quickly patch up whatever cracks might appear, and I disturbed it now, though not without misgivings. The ledger was indeed lying under the heap, its binding ragged, some of the pages sticking out, crumpled and thick with mortar. "I knew I'd find it," I declared.

Moshe caught hold of the ledger, and without a thought for the filth that was getting on the sleeves of his white shirt, cradled it in his arms as though he were saving a child from a burning house. Bilha was waiting for him at the door to the roof, all dressed.

"Wait, Mr. Kattan," Rachel said, "I'll wrap it in a sheet." She meant the ledger. I didn't see how she could wrap the ledger in a sheet without exposing her body to Mr. Kattan—unless she was just teasing? Fortunately, Kattan has no time for such games, and now he was running down the stairs, with his heavy shoes thumping—surrounded by the light but close patter of Bilha's three or four pairs of shoes—and coughing dryly. I hadn't heard him coughing when he came in.

Rachel laughed.

"I wonder whether he's taken home a couple of these ants in his throat," I said to myself, and hurried to my post.

Chapter X

My wife Rachel's little tribute to the ants—I trick the ants that trick me—Brief cease-fires—My wife Rachel suckles and I suck—Man's advantage over the ant.

Two, three, perhaps four days after that visit, in the middle of the day, I awoke with a start with my left hand on the supporting wall I was just then building and my right hand on my knee. For a moment I panicked; I hurriedly picked up half-bricks and ran to stack them in the corners of the room, ready to stop up the dangerous cracks. But soon I relaxed; I even smiled to myself. What had frightened me was the sudden silence. I had worried for a moment that I might have gone deaf.

But I had just imagined it. After all, my sense of hearing was what had woken me the moment the gnawing had stopped and the silence began. And the silence was nothing but a slight pause, two blinks perhaps, in the work—a stage completed, a change of shift, or something of the kind—and immediately the walls were humming with activity again. The direction and sound of some of the lower tones helped me to calculate the location of the vanguard: about three arms' lengths from the concrete support that runs through the kitchen wall. That support and the one in the hallway wall are actually the two main pillars on which the roof of our house rests. By the sound of it, there was no reason for immediate worry. My hearing had become so acute that I think I could have told the ant foreman exactly in what sector of the wall their workers were wasting precious public time in forbidden antenna-gossip.

All in all, things weren't too bad; one might even say they were fairly okay. There was no urgency about the work now and we could take long rests. And since we didn't work much and allowed ourselves to sleep for extended periods, it was only rarely that we felt hungry. Then my wife would run on tiptoe—not without first giving me a questioning look, and my encouraging her with a raised eyebrow—across the sunny roof, pick up the dish our neighbor Bilha, who had not forgotten us, good soul that she was, had pushed under the door, and return blinking to the comforting twilight of the main room. And we would eat cheese sandwiches and leave the dessert in its cups. I didn't ask what my wife did with those cups of dessert. But I knew. She put them in the kitchen on the drainboard and the ants ate the dessert—that was her little tribute. And I could only smile.

It made them—the ants—remarkably broad-minded. They didn't climb on the bed while I was lying on it. They didn't attack me during my short naps. They always took care to walk around my feet, even if it meant they had to detour, which is no small matter for them. Of course, runners or couriers must only take the shortest paths. Thus, they climb up my bare foot on one side and down the other. I didn't interfere with them—no, not me. That much I had learned from my experience with this mighty and efficient species. (Their efficiency, in particular, I am sure, has no like in the mammalian world. They even turn obstacles to their advantage. Two ants hurrying about their business might suddenly meet on a narrow path, crash into each other, tie themselves and their loads into a knot, and then suddenly you'll see them forge ahead side by side, pulling and carrying their joint load at a great speed, like a well-trained team of mules.) Actually, I was grateful that they didn't make use of my naps to burrow a straight—that is to say, more economical—passage right *through* my foot.

So there was actually a kind of unspoken agreement between us, a negative one, you might say, about what not to do, but an agreement all the same. In all other respects I had to be very careful.

Those cracks, for example. I realized that here there was room for letting the ants seem to have their way. After all, they didn't want it to be seen how far they had progressed with their work, and every crack, crevice, gap was information, valuable information. They understood this perfectly well: they were so cautious, in fact, that though their tunnels led straight to the drainboard, the only way they would come to eat their dessert, to grease their armor with its fat, to gain new strength, was by a long, roundabout route, through a visible slit below the rotting frame of the kitchen window.

I pretended that I had not caught on to the trick. That was why I didn't stop up that crack below the kitchen window. On the other hand, I am very careful when it comes to filling other cracks. Here is my strategy: as I hear the crumbling growing louder somewhere in a wall, I prepare myself a piece of brick, moist mortar, and a trowel and wait for the breakthrough. The moment the wall cracks, I stand ready to close it up with the rapid movements of a skilled builder, and so the ants that patrol inside the wall don't have a chance to notice that I've learned the location of one of their reconnaissance squads. It's a fascinating life, really.

My wife helps me. From time to time she draws my attention to a fissure, crack, or gap that is about to develop. Not with words—for some time now we have stopped communicating with words, so as not to dull the sharpness of our hearing. Nor is there need for words: I read the movements of her lips and follow the direction of her eyes.

The two of us, my wife Rachel and I, enjoy long, refreshing periods of relaxation. When the lines of light between the slats of the closed shutters fade, I give a little pull at the shutter cord and the intervals widen and become lookout slits. The two of us, my wife and I, each stand on a brick—the window is high—and put our eyes to one of the slits and look out at the sea. And we speak from the fullness of our hearts, like poets, with proper pauses between the words:

"The sea—on fire—"

"The sea—in flood—"

"The sea—on fire—on fire—"

"The sea—in flood—in flood—"

We scan the words, with proper pauses, with the proper modulation of our voices, so as not to allow the tautness of our listening to slacken, which in our situation would be suicidal. Then I leave from the window, my heart breaking; I kneel down, embrace my wife's knees and press my head into her groin. And my wife goes down on her knees opposite mine and places the nipples of her breasts in my mouth—this is the closest contact we now have—and I suck greedily at her hard, dry breasts. Nothing moves in my wife's body. She kneels frozen on her knees, beautiful, icy, dripping cold mercy unselfishly into my mouth, my throat, the sinews of my body, filling me with the venom of life. Her ears are listening—only in her ears does the blood pulse. She listens. I know that she listens; this is why I can indulge in the mercy of sucking for a while.

"God," I said silently. "You have given man feeling. And what have You given the ant? Only labor, labor. It is a lie to say that the ant makes itself a kingdom in one cubit of soil. Even at this moment they are burrowing ahead, scraping, breaking, drilling, and gnawing, conquering yet a little more space within the walls of my house . . ."

At that thought I jumped to my feet, and so did my wife. And amid the darkness that suddenly filled the room, we hurried to light a candle.

INTERLUDE

Why do the flying ants keep to such low altitudes? Let me propose an answer of my own to that question, an answer in the form of a question: Why should they? What does Don Quixote, knightliest of all knights, say? "It did him harm when the ant grew wings." The question resembles another: Why do the ants not raise their heads to see the world? They don't need to, as I've already explained, and we would be greatly surprised to see those ants, whose beauty is wholly functional, waste their time on beauty of a different order. Thus the wings help the two sexes meet for coupling; afterward, they fall off. Which, it is said, also relates to an ancient tale.

When God created the ants, he gave them long wings. And so the ants flew, near the sun, enjoying the radiance and beauty of creation. But having radiance and beauty in abundance, they began to despise it and lapsed into dreary idleness and terrible boredom. Up rose the Queen of the Ants and with her own mouth trimmed her wings, leaving only about one third for the coupling flight. Seeing this, the other ants followed suit; and since then, say the wise men who know the tongues of all creatures, there are no longer synonyms for "idleness" and "boredom" in the language of the ants.

Chapter XI

The ant that was out of line, and its end—My wife as executioner—
The many uses of the mortal remains—
Some legends and traditions

The glands that work my emotions must not have completely dried up yet. They still secrete strange feelings, humanistic poisons—relics of infancy, the age of milk. It can't be helped: we have been suckled on milk instead of steel, for our sins. I beat my breast in penitence, but I cannot deny my heart—and my heart aches for that ant and its frightful end. I should pass over this story in silence, but I cannot. So I will tell about the ant that found itself out of line.

I was on my way through the kitchen and saw a great commotion on the drainboard. On the flat square of the drainboard, which has an area of a billion square ant heads, according to their standard unit of measure, something like a parade or a procession or a demonstration seemed to be taking place. I couldn't see the reviewing stand, but it was easy to guess that it was inside the wall, behind one of the arched openings. But on the great square—aside from those powerful-looking ants with bent heads, apparently the ushers, that were posted, each in its place, all around the perimeter of the spectacle, antennae up and jaws bared—everything else was in motion.

And what motion! Ranks upon ranks of ants flowing out of an arched opening in the wall, passing over the marble expanse and flowing into yet another opening in the wall. It was marvelous to see the strange and yet economical order of their movements. Regiments, brigades, camps, trotting along in unison, block by block, loading sugar without breaking their well-tempered steps. Clearly, a great feat of organizational acumen. For every file of runners was also a file of lifters. Grains of sugar were strewn in abundance all over the drainboard—I don't know who had left them there, perhaps my wife!—and this was their procedure:

The hosts of runners, moving in columns, advance through stationary columns; at some signal, the moving columns, as one, grasp the white, glistening sugar in their jaws and continue their precise motion. Shortly afterward, at some signal that I cannot perceive, the stationary columns in turn grasp sugar granules, as one, and load them on the backs of the running ants—an enormous army forging ahead with divine confidence and geometrical precision, each of its units carrying two large grains of sugar. One can easily imagine that this is the only way my ants know how to salute—sugar between jaws and a white grain of sugar on the back—their generals on the hidden stand.

From time to time, once every few seconds, the columns of runners come to a dead halt; the lifting ranks have already assumed the same confident steady flow, while the columns that have halted take over the abrupt cadence of lifting and loading; and so on, and so forth.

I didn't manage to discover whether they were part of a huge army marching on and on, with the vanguard not knowing of the rear, and while the first brigades were already back at work, butting and cutting, cracking and grinding in the twisted cavities of the wall, the brigades in the rear were still parading their serried ranks; or whether it was perhaps a single corps marching around in a circle, part inside the wall and part outside on the marble square.

I wouldn't find out; it isn't easy to distinguish one ant from another. But how glorious was that army! A thousand two-way gears, a giant grinding machine of serrated strips moving against each other, a black river set with silver blades—my heart overflowed with fear and admiration . . . Enough! I shall never be able to describe so great a spectacle. A thought in motion! My eyes could not encompass it. For relief I turned to an ant I had just then discovered out of the line, alone, miserable, but so wonderful, so small in its loneliness and so great in its hurried, confused movements . . .

How had it dropped out of line? I don't know. Suddenly there it was, outside. Perhaps it had lost step, tripped over its own legs, and was not admitted again by the closed ranks. Perhaps it had tried to return and the proud ushers had pushed it out.

The ant looked here and there. For a while it ran around about the parade ground, with its legs brushing against each other—taught to run in the ranks, it didn't know where to make its legs work now that it was alone. It almost twisted its back, poor little thing, as it bent its head until the joints cracked, left and right, in a hopeless search—and the sugar granule all the time weighing down on its back.

At last it recovered a little and came to the end of the marble square. And there it stood and saw in the middle of a giant canyon—a kind of square crater with steep sides—a tiny hill of soil with its slopes dipping into some small lakes of water divided by tongues of glazed earth. Out of the hill a cactus proudly grew, with dark green, juicy, fleshy leaves, one leaf growing from the other and reaching up and sideways, a coarse plant that had declined to produce thin lacy fronds and pliant branches waving in the wind. Instead, it grew thick leaves like common working hands, their skin all wrinkles and thorns.

A cactus in the sink—how come? Rachel, of course. One day she had seen a thin stalk rising from the drain. Apparently it had taken root somewhere in the U-bend below the sink. Some of the dust the ants had chewed up must have lodged there; in any case, the sink could no longer be used. It was clogged with dust. Not that we needed it. The little food we needed Bilha gave us, sometimes in a covered dish under the door, sometimes, when Rachel consented, from Bilha's own hands. So my wife had collected a little of the dust the ants had ground in the sink and laid a cactus leaf on it. Again my wife had been right when she assumed the ants' dust was highly fertile. The tap dripped perhaps at the rate of a drop an hour. But that was enough for a many-leafed cactus to grow within a few days—juicy, angry, but beautiful. Rachel looked at it from time to time. It seemed to prosper under her looks. I never understood why she wanted a cactus. The top leaf bent sideways, flat like an altar. It was like an altar. It was very prickly. Its hooked tip pointed upward. The lost ant ran down the smooth white wall of the crater, hurried to the tongue of dry land that separated the lakes, didn't stop to rest in the giant shadows of the cactus that floated in the water, and immediately began the climb, with the two sugar beads still loaded on its body. Some internal process, enthusiasm perhaps, seemed to propel its legs, which didn't get in each other's way now, and moved rapidly, as if floating, as if they carried neither body nor load.

It clambered up the first leaf, then up the second. Pierced all over its body, it stopped to rest on the third leaf, near its goal, trying to pull the thorns from its body and to lick its wounds. But when it was high up on the third leaf and saw the whole wide crater lying below it, the shadows of the leaves bathing in the lakes and the bank of the drainboard-plain sloping down, it immediately stopped treating its wounds and climbed on. The sugar beads weighed it down, but it carried them, a prisoner of habit, one between its mandibles and the other on its back. From time to time it disappeared among the twisting paths of the cactus, and I thought, not without concern, that I might not see it again. High on the next leaf it reappeared, bruised and full of energy, and there it raised its head high like a charger stretching its proud neck.

The crater was already far away; the giant assembly whose movements seemed from that distance like a loom at work, warp into woof, occupied only a corner of the wide space. Then the ant dropped the grain of sugar from its jaws.

With its mandibles free, the little body leaped ahead, drawn upward with new strength, looking as though it would never tire. Between poisonous spearheads it ran over hills, jumped over pits, and there it was finally on the flat, altar like leaf. Swiftly it ran across and at its end, high up on its erect finger, it stopped; its head straightened up, extended. What the ant saw there, I do not know. The lines of the landscape, the low hills, the lakes, the walls of the crater, the warp and woof of the armies on the marble square, the rough, cold, wide walls riven by the holes, their innards of tunnels and cracks, and beyond the glass planes bands of blue blinking with distant lights. It stood perfectly still; its rounded head, glistening in the light, stretched as though to inhale the sights.

Then it dropped the second sugar grain from its back and its body leaped forward in a magnificent, free, glorious leap, its hind legs last to leave the pinnacle of the altar; and as it sketched an arc through the air, its head shone, glowed high in its trajectory.

Yes, that was how the little ant that got out of line looked, before it fell to the ground. Or rather, into the little muddy lake. The ant did not die. The alert messengers of the army did their duty and collected it from the water. They also carefully collected the two sugar beads the wayward ant had dropped.

Yes. The wayward ant—its fate was sealed. They laid it at the end of the drainboard square, on the edge of the crater.

It didn't even resist. Harsh is the vengeance of the ant tribe, but even the life of the rebel is not outside the law. No one took private revenge. Harsh is the vengeance of the ant tribe, but not excessive.

There was, for example, the pulling method in which the ant is pulled from both ends, like the rope in a tug-of-war, until it's torn apart, or rather disjointed—for the ant's body, as we know, is all joints—at the weakest places, namely where the different segments are connected. The parts of the body come in useful, each in its own way; the head as a sledge, the jaws as extension levers, the belly as a mobile honey container; what the intermediate joints, the antennae, and the legs are used for, I did not see—I'm sure they don't go to waste either.

Then there was the pecking method. This method may be applied in different degrees of severity, from pecking out part or all of the condemned's eyes to amputating its antennae—which deprives the ant of all sensations except those of pain and hunger. But since it no longer has any means of orientation, it only runs about for a while until it dies of hunger. And here it should be noted that none of the others ever touch it until it dies a natural death. Then its parts are used in the same way as with the pulling method. Harsh is the vengeance of the ant tribe, but orderly.

Harsh is the vengeance of the ant tribe, but not lacking in a sense of humor. Meaning, of course, organized humor, or entertainment. An ancient tale—I forget where I read it—tells of an ancient ant ruler who ordered the lateral, sideways-looking eyes of his own body to be pecked out with all its subjects watching. This spectacle became so popular that the day was proclaimed eye-pecking day for all time. Another ruler gave orders—and, later this became a primary feature of their architecture—to pave the gates of their tunnels and passages with rebels' heads, thereby achieving three lofty ends in one single stroke:

Punishment of the rebels,

Strengthening of the gates,

Architectural beauty.

But back to our ant, whom we left lying, alone and trembling, on the edge of the great crater, awaiting its fate, but still whole, yes, whole in all its limbs. The great moment, the moment of its flight, still quivered in its body. Had they forgotten it? Had they forgiven it?

As these thoughts went through my head, I already knew that there was no hope of this. The solution of the riddle came from an unexpected direction. My wife Rachel. She walked in, dressed in black, glistening net, stepped up to the drainboard, caught the ant between two fingers, did something with two other fingers, and when she put the ant back on the drainboard—all this with breathtaking speed—it was already deprived of its mandibles and antennae, and my wife hissed furiously: "Parasite, parasite."

We know what came next. Now, while we mourn its fate, let us ask what was done with its body after its death.

Let us turn over the pages of the calendar—one of the few objects the ants do not want to devour, even though I often find them walking between its pages. Not many more such pages are left till the one with the fort that rises proudly above the chasm, with the face of a Roman boy on one side, beautiful as Rachel, and on the other side a maiden dancing in the vineyards, clothed in white, also like Rachel. Well then, there is a wall in that picture, half breached. And in front of the breach, a row of fellows dressed in togas are pushing and pulling at a black iron beam hanging from ropes—the famous ram for breaching ramparts. I do not know whether the ants saw it there and imitated it. What they use for a ram is the body of an ant coated with honey, hardened with a mixture of secretions of which the formula, for all I know, has not yet been unriddled by science.

A sharp eye will immediately discern the ant-like shape of the ram in the picture. This leads us to the hypothesis that the Romans, outstanding technicians and organizers that they were, had learned to cast their rams from the form of the ant, which has always been an example of solid and at the same time economically streamlined structure. The possibility cannot be excluded that the Romans—whom history knows as poor inventors and originators in comparison with their great talent for adopting the ideas and discoveries of others—learned the art of the ram from the ants.

Note the appearance of the ant: the perfect ovality of its segments; its large, solid head—a natural sledge; the central segments that extend leverage and offer natural hand holds; and finally, the long belly which in movement converts the whole body into one mass of energy. I have not seen the ants butting with those hard black bodies of theirs against the last of the concrete blocks and brick barriers that remain in the walls of my apartment. But I have heard them. I have heard the concrete blocks crumbling, the brick barriers splitting, cracking, and falling away, and the walls of the building opening, gap after gap, lending to its ultimate ruin. I have heard the sound of the ram.

What did the rebel ant think in its last moments? I am sure it didn't consider the honor of its nice, solid body being made into a battering ram. Probably it thought about the wide open spaces it had seen in that very fleeting moment of its flight.

INTERLUDE

With my own eyes I have seen an ant rear up and, with a lunge of its mandible that would have put a fencing champion to shame, behead a spider that had tried to enter one of the ants' openings in the wall. I saw no preparations for this attack. I did not see the mandible brought into position, and yet the severed head was already stuck on its point, was quickly being carried to its destination while being sucked dry of the nourishing juices that it contained.

The facts force me to confess our limitations. How can I catch the movements of an ant's jaw cutting, decapitating, chewing, chopping, perforating, boring, and cracking—and those are only a few of its activities—if my eye cannot discern any movement briefer than the sixteenth part of a second; how can I hear the sound of their alarms and excursions of assembly and dismissal, of song and hymn, of judgment and condemnation, of law and commandment, if my ear can only perceive a frequency of sixteen to twenty thousand vibrations per second, something even the most degenerate lapdog would regard as pathetic? With bowed head I join all the others, scientists great and small, and chalk it up to the ants' secret language—which is merely an admission of failure.

Chapter XII

Metamorphosis of Rachel—A madcap game my wife plays makes the supporting wall collapse. The game excites me—We now have a dream in common—"Ants over you, Jacob!"—I whet a knife to slaughter my wife Rachel.

My wife Rachel did not seem upset at all. The white of her skin peeped innocent and pure through the little squares of the black netting that covered her body.

She stood and looked at me with a cold, mysterious, hypnotizing stare, half a second or half a minute, just long enough for her to come up with a new dirty trick. Then she burst into a barefoot gallop from the kitchen to the main room, with her voice ringing like the windowpane when the sea wind knocks at it. I ran after her, of course. I wanted to do something to her, to punish her. My flesh was full of the scars of my humiliation. Even the netting on her skin, which she had pulled on like a stocking from the soles of her feet up to her shoulders, had become a manifesto of insult and treason. Ants by the dozen scurried between the threads of the net that barred her so painfully desired body from me, her husband. Just when it seemed that her heart had turned, however little, in my favor, her latest behavior now cut into me even more deeply than ever.

Perhaps it had something to do with the swelling of the walls.

It started like the smallpox. A few blisters came up on the kitchen wall next to where the concrete pillar presumably runs through it, and after that I saw them everywhere, some large as a bean, others like water bubbles about to burst. But amazingly, they did not burst; what's more, they stretched and spread sideways, clutched each other, merged, disappeared into each other, and then we had whole sections of wall, perforated and blistered, with a bright gray color like quicksilver. I knew, this was what I felt in my heart, this was the beginning of the end. I do not know what Rachel thought, but the rapid change in her behavior told its own story.

As the walls began to swell, her half-asleep, devout-dreamy mood changed into a kind of strange nightmarish vitality; like a tigress that is weaned and suddenly feels the strength of her teeth, like a virgin nun who realizes one day that the God over her altar is male. Her flesh seemed to awake to life, but not to me. She would bolt without warning, as if she was having a fit, as if she was being stung or tickled by those ants who were strolling through the thousands of gateways of her black netting with a familiarity that made me jealous. In vain I would run her, chase her, something at which I had never been any good and which more than once brought me to the floor with a thump, accompanied by peals of laughter from my wife and the mortification of my aching body.

What to do to Rachel in her net armor? All my tension and desire melted and I dragged myself to the large calendar in the kitchen, looked at the magic page and read on it: "New House." This ancient promise returned a little strength to my loins; I lowered my eyes before Rachel, and Rachel, perhaps tired, perhaps she must rest a little from her wild galloping, closed her eyes for a few poor miserable caresses, disgusting leavings from the ants' table. Ah, what hope was there in this devil's game!

Now, after seeing with my own eyes how my wife Rachel executed a sentence of death by torture, in cold blood, on that poor ant, a terrible anger flared up in me. This time, I said to myself, I will make her pay. So eager was I that I heard the gallop of a knightly steed in the stamping of my heavy feet. They kicked up great clouds of dust, my feet, and this only thickened the concealing screen of dust in which Rachel moved, in which she held back her laughter, letting out a peal from time to time, like a misleading call in a game of hide and seek. I have not yet explained the latest change in our situation. This was the dust from an actual collapse, but not of one of the house's walls, not yet—meanwhile they exhaled denser and denser clouds of fine dust that looked as transparent as silk when a sudden ray of light from the shutter hit them. The screen of dust in which my wife maneuvered rose from the collapse of the supporting wall that I had hurriedly built with a bare minimum of mortar between its bricks, so that it could take the weight of the ceiling when the hall wall, through which ran one of the concrete supports that held up the house, would finally be chewed up.

I ran into it with the whole weight of my body, without hesitating, and the force with which the wall hit me back was equal to that of my assault—you may imagine the restrained, disciplined satisfaction of the ant army as their enemy did their work for them—I galloped to the bed, underneath which came the sounds of my wife Rachel's laughter, and just managed to catch hold of her heel and tear some of the netting off her body, and perhaps some flesh of the heel as well. She rose in the air like a flame. "You're hurting me," she screamed, half in pain, half in jest, as she landed in the corner of the room, where she tried to raise a new dust screen between us by scratching at the wall with her nails; as I chased her, it had not escaped me that her dragons' teeth, the clever interplay between the crooked cracks in the wall and the lines of my wife's paintbrush, seemed to be grinding out the dust themselves, filtering a shield of dust over the body of my traitorous wife.

"Now even the dragons' teeth will not save her from me," I said to myself. I felt the exultation of a beast of prey smelling blood. I grasped the flesh of her thigh and tore the netting off it, while four wild legs—Rachel's and mine—stamped from our room to the hall, from the hall to the roof and from the roof again to the hall and on to our room; the bed caught us like an altar of lust.

Rachel fell on the bed, clasping the pillow, waiting and laughing, and her body, scalding in its sweat, rose under me in fire. I threshed, trod, twisted the sinews of her white flesh, stretched her neck, bruised her thighs—in short, I did all the things lust reinforced by terrible anger can do . . . Ah, God! You know how I had been driven to it. Suddenly, my face felt her eyes.

One point needs explaining. True, I was again taking my wife Rachel by force. But there all resemblance between what was happening now and what had happened that Sabbath night ended. Then, her body had been dead and her heart full of disgust. For hours afterward the water had run down her body and it had seemed there was not water enough in the pipes to rinse off all the dirt. This time it was a battle, a battle which had been preceded by battle cries and challenges; this time, her flesh was not wholly indifferent.

Which made my defeat more painful still.

Yes. Rachel was not with me even now. I beat the air. Her eyes told me of my humiliation. Her eyes, wide, alert, were elsewhere; a light-greenish glow, icy cold, the look of a tiger in the jungle (eyes pregnant with danger and mystery, within which her pupils grew long in narrow slits). Yes, it could not be doubted—I was being mocked.

And what in her did not mock, listened. There was an unusual silence. All traffic in the walls must have come to a halt. Even when the work was eventually resumed, I still heard that threatening silence. Were the ants listening? All the time I was kneading my wife Rachel's body, were the ants listening to my wife and was my wife listening to the ants? Perhaps they were conversing? I would not be surprised if the large stinging ant I just had removed from the corner of my mouth had come to gather a little lover's foam to test it in the laboratory inside the wall . . . I had no strength left for laughter, let alone for anger. My wife was already changing: throwing her old dress away and putting on a new one, a whole new set of black netting she pulled out from under the heap of sheets she no longer needed in the corner of the wardrobe.

It would be wrong to think that I didn't get a certain pleasure out of this new situation. I must have: I returned with renewed energy to building my supporting walls—after neglecting them for so long in my wretched defeatism—only for my wife Rachel to rise against them and destroy them and so I might pursue her again in red-hot anger until I could again slake my lust on her. This hellish little game that slowly exhausted my body also exhausted my attention and my entire conscience. Hours passed, entire hours, in which I was unaware of the sounds of the ants' work. In alarm I again tested the sharpness of my hearing and found, to my joy, that it was no less keen, that it had still not deserted me. My ears, trained to receive and record everything from the fine sound of the gnawing of the youngest recruits to the drilling and cracking of the ants with the enormous jaws, and the whole scale of intermediate sounds too, had lost nothing of their sensitivity. What was happening was that these sounds still entered my ears but no longer could penetrate my exhausted, sleepy consciousness. It was a relaxing but dangerous state.

One day I couldn't take any more and called to my wife, who was busy in some lethargic swoon with her eyes wide open:

"Rachel, which side are you on, mine or theirs?"

Rachel remained silent and did not even blink.

"Answer me!" I shouted.

Then I saw her stare come alive. She looked at me with distant, clear, transparent, but not bottomless eyes. I saw down into them. I drowned in their depth, as in a lake of liquid ice—but I could not see all the way through them. Then, there was her voice, soft and caressing:

"What will our new house be like, Jacob?" Those words, the sound of them alone, was enough to make me happy. I was moonstruck.

"It will have a glass dome," I daydreamed.

"Make it tall, Jacob, tall."

"And I'll make it wide, Rachel, wide."

"Why make it wide, Jacob, why make it wide?"

"Half on the hillside and half on the sea, Rachel."

"What will our new house be like, Jacob?"

"It will have a glass dome, Rachel, it will have a glass dome," I daydreamed.

This brief dialogue robbed me of my remaining strength and wakefulness. Dazed, paralyzed, sleepy, surrendering to all ruin, I would sink into dreams for whole hours, days perhaps. I don't know how often this dialogue was repeated, but I know that after it ended I was always, inevitably, overcome by sleep. I lost my sense of day and night. Our two clocks had stopped; the fine dust that seeped in everywhere must have halted their hands. I could not remember when I had last asked the time. If a feeling of discomfort overcame me in a moment of dreamy wakefulness, some irritating reminder of some work I had to do, it only made me sink back faster into my lethargy. Till one day my wife Rachel frightened me with a shout of alarm:

"The ants, Jacob, the house is falling!"

Thunderstruck, I jumped off the bed. After I had come to myself and saw that the house was still standing, I hurried to the cracks, to stop them, and in maddened haste I built a new support wall. A wall. Let there be something solid in the house. And then Rachel started the chasing game again, and the wall would come down, and our galloping would raise shivers of desire in my flesh. And eat away my strength.

My wife Rachel, when she saw how this game of hers—the terrifying midnight cry of "Ants" and all that followed—caught hold of me, terrified me, how it roused me from even the deepest sleep, must have decided to improve on it. What did she do? On the same spot where she used to put a crumb of mud while I slept, in days past—namely, between my upper lip and nostrils—she now put a dozen ants, strong and spoiling for a fight like wild animals, as an overture to her nightly alarm cries. As I ran to save what I could, the ants were already eating my lips, my nose, and already I saw the terror of annihilation before my eyes; I ran and ranted all over the apartment, pulling down and ruining more of the place than I had built and reinforced. Till I decided to put an end to it.

It was a little tool that put the idea into my head. A scout knife. It was lying quietly, almost waiting, on a shelf in my tool chest, and my hand twitched toward it. There was a dark stain on its curved blade, not rust, perhaps old blood. I wondered why I hadn't thought of this before. Above my wife Rachel's tiger eyes her neck was thin as a swan's. I don't know how but everything had built up to this terrible sentence:

I must cut her throat up on the support wall.

It made hope rush into my heart. Suddenly I knew that her blood would strengthen the support wall. Perhaps it would demoralize the ants. Perhaps it would frighten them off, perhaps, who knew, it would push back the invasion entirely.

I whetted the knife under Rachel's eyes. I got so much pleasure from that. I spat lavishly on the flat top of the support wall and drew the blade of the knife over it. The blade was already fairly sharp, but, yes, I got a great deal of pleasure from the whetting. Rachel stared at the knife—bewitched, wordless. Its blade was slightly curved, its edge thin, you could split a hair in the air with it. And still I did not stop whetting it. Except for the dramatic pauses. In these pauses I put the knife in its sheath and the sheath in the belt of my pants. There was some difficulty finding the right moments. It was a powerful weapon, perhaps my last chance. I had to obtain the maximum effect with it. And it seemed as though my wife Rachel was doing all she could to make this easy for me.

She offered me so many opportunities. Often she dozed with her throat bare before my eyes, rising only to arouse my anger with her provocative galloping about, destroying the support wall on the way. She would wake me in perfect fits of fright, and as I drew the knife from its sheath in a murderous frenzy, I would see that the support wall, which I had sworn to make the altar of her sacrifice, had again become a heap of ruins. So, again I would build it, again I would whet the knife on it, and she, my wife Rachel, would again stare bewitched at the knife.

Once, after I had forced my lust on her, and her eyes were far away, and the sudden silence had worked its evil in the wall, and those slits of mockery were in her eyes, I said to myself: This is the moment. Her throat, her bare, bent throat, was soft as down. Her open eyes didn't move as I passed one hand over her throat, with the knife already shining in the other—as her voice rose, soft and caressing, pouring out sweet drunkenness:

"What will our house be like, Jacob?"

I was moonstruck: "It will have a glass dome," I daydreamed.

"Make it tall, tall, Jacob."

"I'll make it wide too, Rachel, wide."

"Why make it wide, Jacob, why make it wide?"

"Half on the hillside and half on the sea, Rachel."

"What will our house be like, Jacob?"

"It will have a glass dome, Rachel, it will have a glass dome."

INTERLUDE

Let me try to describe in all its beauty the head of the bronze ant. Its shape is oval. It rises and swells from the place where it is joined to the dorsal segment, in a smooth, strong line, gleaming like hammered, beaten steel, graceful in its broad curve, storing strength in silence, resting in its energy, and suddenly, out of the stillness of this restrained strength, a free flow of slanting lines, convex, severe, bursts forth powerful, and encloses the mandibles. It is a head that stretches in battle like a horse's neck, gleaming in the light like a mane. As the ant uses its jaw, as a sword or battering ram, the head stretches like a lever that terminates at its sharp horn. As it rears, its head vibrates as though to retain a mighty neigh. Then it resembles a horse about to fly; but having no wings, the head swells in jubilant quivers as if it wanted to imbibe the air of the whole universe in one breath. In those moments the ant, whose black body glistens like basalt, resembles lava: congealed without and red-hot within . . .

Hell! I meant to describe an ant and have instead described a kind of divine horse . . .

Chapter XIII

I raise the knife against Rachel and drive it into a piece of wood—
I carve a sculpture of an ant—The ants cut off the power—
Questions I did not ask—Rachel lights candles—The ant sculpture
looks at our love—Sweet dreams of perdition.

I carved a man—that was how it looked from the back—and he had six legs. I have never carved wood or done handicrafts. My fingers are no good for fine work: ten houses of concrete and not a single swan's neck. They recoil, perhaps even in fear, from the delicate. They trembled on my wife Rachel's throat. They were strong, though, on the thick, rough wooden handle of the knife.

I sat on the support wall I had just rebuilt and looked at Rachel. Rachel was dozing. She didn't look at me and her eyes weren't mocking. I drew the knife from its sheath and moved toward her. Her eyes were open, perhaps even attentive, but her rhythmic breathing, which sounded like a whispered spell or litany, showed that she was indeed sleeping. I passed my fingers over her long neck without touching it. It seemed endless. I was afraid to touch it. The sound of the ants from the walls was confident now, sometimes drawn out like a trumpet call reverberating all at once in many places. That call roused my hands to action. I swung it forcefully and drove it—the knife—into a thick, short wooden beam that had caught my eye. This piece of wood that I'd taken along for casting girders and had never used—it had split and revealed vein upon vein of white timber free of knots, grains, or other faults. The wall that had been designed to receive my wife Rachel's blood now served me as a workbench. I worked in a fever. But I did not as yet know what I was making.

"What is it?" asked Rachel, her eyes on the object in my hand.

"A horse," I said. I was annoyed and said: "A horse." She looked at me and said, "No." But there was still no mockery in her eyes, rather surprise, wonderment—I almost said mercy, but that couldn't be. Perhaps it was only a mercy that she did not destroy the support wall again, playing catch-me-if-you-can or some other prank, of which there seemed to be no end in my wife's mind . . .

But she was right. It was no horse. From the wooden block, six legs had already begun to emerge. Perhaps a horse with its rider. I didn't know. I worked on the back of the wood. The top of the head was human, a human skull, shorn of ears, suspicious, listening, thinking in terror, but the neck was long and curved like a horse's, again a horse whose neck is thunder and whose snorting is terrible, as the Book says. But Rachel said it was not a horse. I believe I ate a plate of rice my wife Rachel set before me on the support wall, and as the shadows began to hide between the curves of my wood, I knew it was night.

"What is it?"

"A horse."

My wife lit candles, and as the light began caressing the leg joints and belly folds of the carving, she said:

"No, no horse."

There was no electricity in the house now—the ants' work, probably. With a few drilling and cracking operations they had no doubt turned the protective tin conduit and the copper wires into useless slivers of metal. The fact that they had not done it till now must not be ascribed to laziness or thoughtlessness. Very likely they had bided their time. This seemed the right moment to them, as witness their thoroughness: the lighting wires and the appliance wires cut at the same moment. And in the dense darkness of the night the support wall turned into ruins once more without my knowing who had brought it down. Rachel? The ants? The walls of our house were alive with the sound of muffled explosions. I stood naked in the center of our room and imagined myself dreaming myself in the hollow of a giant mountain that was about to fall in.

Is it coming, Rachel, is it coming?

Then I saw Rachel with a lit candle in each hand. She held the candles like a priestess, before her eyes, and the candles shone in her eyes and her mouth was slightly open, perhaps for reciting a prayer. Would the ceiling hit us on some gloomy, dark day? Perhaps in the deep of night? Perhaps in sleep? And if in sleep—is that fair? Perhaps this now was our last rehearsal! Perhaps a "severe warning." But if this was a "severe warning"—was our fate not already written, or rather being written, on the walls of our apartment in crooked lines of cracks and breaches? Your eyes shone, Rachel, while all else was cloaked in darkness—how did your eyes shine? Could you see in the dark, like the ants? How did you know to have candles ready, Rachel, how did you know? All those questions I did not ask.

Rachel fixed the candles to the wall that divides our room from the hall. She let a drop of wax fall and attached a candle to it, let another drop fall and attached another candle, both in cracks in the wall, each candle in its crack.

And suddenly, in this flickering light, I saw that my carving was indeed neither horse nor man. It was black and gleaming. I set fire to the cuttings and splinters that were left of the beam, and with the ash I rubbed the magnificent wooden body that now turned gray and gleamed with a solid gloss.

"It is an ant," my wife said. And I saw that it was truly an ant.

Her eyes glowed and deepened. The slits of pupils widened and exuded the honey of mercy as she went down on her knees and placed my broad, rough hand, the hand that had worked the wood, onto her forehead. Her eyes were on the dark wooden sculpture and she intoned: "Pray!" I murmured something. Rachel slowly rose from her knees, pulled a thread out of the netting she wore, and used it to tie the ant sculpture to the cord of the unlit lamp above the headboard of our bed, so that the proud, magnificent face of the ant would never stop looking aslant at the place where we were to celebrate our ultimate union.

Rachel took off her netting. Her body turned itself toward me, her breasts swelled like two skins of water, sweet and deadly. Three candles now burned with leaping flames, little tongues of fire that grew brighter and paler, rose and fell. The magnificent sculpture swung like a pendulum, to and fro, the jaws of its mouth gleamed, radiated laughter, radiated fear, melted the candle wax.

A sudden, foreign light, which obviously would soon wane and disappear, burst between the slats of the closed shutter. It lit up veil upon veil of shining dust. And after the light—a sound like the galloping of horses on mountain rock, like the far-off clatter of trains.

I awoke from a sweet dream of perdition and saw the Book dropping from Rachel's hand. I picked the Book up and it fell open at the place where a hairpin from Rachel's head was stuck as a marker. I read in a quiet voice that rose as I read on. Tiny grains of dust beat incessantly on the open page:

The appearance of them is as the appearance of horses; and as horsemen, so shall they run. Like the noise of chariots on the mountains shall they leap, like the noise of a flame of fire that devoureth the stubble, as a strong people set in battle array. Before their face the people shall be much pained; all faces shall gather blackness. They shall run like mighty men; they shall climb the wall like men of war; and they shall march every one on his way, and they shall not break their ranks: neither shall one trust another; they shall walk every one in his path; and when they fall upon the sword, they shall not be wounded. They shall run to and fro in the city; they shall run upon the wall, they shall climb up on the houses; they shall enter in it the windows like a thief. The earth shall quake before them; and the heavens shall tremble.

My wife did not sleep. She looked at the sculpture and listened. Then, suddenly, she opened her mouth, widened her lips—and what first looked like a yawn to me turned into a grin. We were both naked and without any shame.

INTERLUDE

I tied a long, thin nylon thread to an ant's belly and let it run into a cavity in the wall. I wanted to find out whether the armies worked together, or separately, each in its own tunnel system.

After perhaps half a minute the ant emerged, and the thread with it, from another crack in the wall. And then, like a joke at my expense, it reappeared, with the thread, once for every two blinks of my terrified eyes, in every split, every crack, every hole in the house. What had I wanted to know—and what did I learn? That a thin shell of plaster protects this house—the roof is heavy and the walls of our apartment are hollow.

Chapter XIV

How shall the voice sound?—The ants' eagerness to finish impresses
me—We do not eat and are not hungry—"One grain is all that holds
each wall"—We are waiting for the sound;
so are the ants—We are happy.

How shall the voice sound?

Both of us, Rachel and I, are waiting for the sound. We know it's not far off. For some time now they have been working steadily, but with less and less noise, as the pockets of resistance shrink, on breaking down the last supports. The sounds of their explosions are no longer muffled, silenced by the twisting tunnels; they come clear as trumpet calls, their echoes make the walls or what remains of them resound—from within.

"How shall the voice sound?" We keep ourselves busy guessing. We know the breaking point isn't far off, and the guessing keeps me from being distracted by other things. Rachel's eyes, as she asks, are transparent green, almost peaceful.

"Like an earthquake," I say.

"Ssst," Rachel giggles subvocally. From the palm of her hand she feeds grains of sugar to a group of ants that gambol at her feet like tiger cubs. Elastic, playful, they move their powerful heads at peculiar angles, pass the rolling grains of sugar to each other in the dust and neigh like young war horses. Rachel reaches her hand out and the cubs run out of it, strong and hungry for play. She produces them by the handful, it's not magic, from the bushes under her arms, from the shady path between her breasts. Now her eyes widen and she says:

"How shall the voice sound?"

I try to frighten her with a long, dull cry like a shofar blast that I make with my windpipe and nose. I trumpet the sound into her bare belly—for some time now we have been doing without clothes—and we intertwine in abrupt, muted laughter. We are very careful. Gripping each other with our teeth and nails we listen so as not to be surprised by the sound when it comes. Armed but weak, we crawl along in the brown dust, throw ourselves against the walls, and with dull groans we scratch them, scratch at the walls.

The dust falls, fine as transparent cloth. Rachel moves within it as in royal robes. Now they are grinding the stuff of the wall thoroughly, into a ghostly thinness. Before, they worked a little roughly, impatiently, against time, but now they are careful—and as an old builder I appreciated it—and are dotting every i. The sounds of the gnawing, too, are well blended, rise and fall in a cheerful but not frivolous rhythm, strong but not proud, like a hymn. Rachel's eyes are listening. "That is not the sound," she whispers.

Rachel's eyes are large, clinging, burning with wonder. Her skin is transparent, stretched over her bones like an eardrum. We couple slowly and over longer spans of time. The sound must not catch us at a moment of ecstatic forgetfulness. We barely have flesh on our bones from which to escape into ecstatic forgetfulness anyway. Our eyes burn, our bones flutter beneath our skin.

I am not hungry—and I don't remember when we last ate. From time to time my wife puts one grain of sugar on my tongue and one on hers, and each of us tries, using our tongues alone, to capture both grains for ourselves, until they melt. A wonderful game! And so distracting. The fine dust, when the light catches it, is spread all over our naked, clinging bodies like a cloak of transparent gauze, highlighting our wonderful, shameless nakedness. The pages of the Book—which have been torn out and crumpled between the contortions of our bodies and surround us by the dozen, insisting on covering our shame with their meaningless rustle, their vulgar touch—we wave them away, everywhere, anywhere. Then we hold still and look at the ant sculpture. I count Rachel's ribs through her white, smooth, silky, transparent skin. Like the insides of the walls through their shells of plaster. I count them with my lips, with my nose, with my tongue. They push at her skin like puffs of air, like bubbles of sound burning inside the shell of the house. I drink from Rachel's breasts, which swell and swell as her body shrinks and shrinks.

"Do you hear . . . Jacob?" Yes, the rattle of wheels comes clambering up, and crrrrack, the rattle of wheels is cut off.

"How shall the voice sound?" I ask in a burst of fright.

Rachel lays two fingers on my lips to silence me, and her voice falls strangely into what sounds like ragged words from an old worn-out song:

"What will . . . our house be like? . . ."

"What house . . . Rachel? . . ." my lips murmur.

"What did you say . . . Jacob? . . ."

"A dome . . . a dome . . ."

"Of glass . . . of glass . . ."

"What did you say . . . Rachel? . . ."

"The voice—Jacob—how shall the voice sound?" Rachel crossed her hands over her breasts.

I jumped up and ran to the walls. No, I did not run, I folded up, went down to the floor, crawled. I no longer had the strength to run. I crawled fast, listening, from wall to wall. Rachel's eyes followed me, very large, now filling half her face. I came back and reported to Rachel in a triumphant voice:

"One grain is all that is holding up each wall."

"One grain?" Rachel asked in a whisper—and the light-green of her eyes flared up in green fire. We rose and sang in unison:

> *One grain is all that holds each wall,*
> *One grain is all that holds each wall.*

And as we shouted "Wall," we ran, holding each other, against the kitchen wall. Nothing happened. Perhaps we scratched a little whitewash off, perhaps not; we had grown very weak, our bodies barely obeyed us. We dragged ourselves back to the bed. There we knelt, facing the bronze sculpture with the bronze face, terrible behind its kindness, marvelously arbitrary. Rachel laid her hand on my forehead and murmured something. I laid my hand on her forehead and murmured something along with her. In response came the murmur of the ants, and a flaming sunset, like one of the vividly colored pictures from the kitchen calendar, broke between the slats of the shutter. Something moved faintly in my brain, and as fast as my weakened limbs allowed, I crawled to the kitchen and tore off the picture of the rock.

"The sea . . . the sea . . ." my wife whispered, her eyes far away.

Through the glistening ashes—that was how the drifting dust looked in the dying light—before we mounted our couch of expectation, we still saw the tail end of the calendar page, with "NEW HOUSE" on it in dust-covered capitals, rolled into a tube like a ram's horn, being dragged into the wall.

Tonight we will not have candles to give us light. There are no candles left. We had imagined that candlelight helped us to hear; now we realize that we don't even need the candlelight to see. The dust that sifts down incessantly looks in the dark of the night like glowing ash. Our eyes have set it alight. Rachel's eyes shine on my face, her pupils like mirrors. I see myself inside her eyes. We sit motionless and listen. A rolling echo sends a shiver through our flesh, an echo that must grow into a blast from a horn.

But the horn call does not come. "What are they waiting for?" "The same thing as us," whispers Rachel.

We wrap ourselves together. The skin of Rachel's body is snow white, white and smooth and transparent, like a wedding gown. Above us hangs a canopy of glowing ashes. Rachel's eyes burn. And inside her eyes, she and I—on our knees, embracing, heads raised, skin crawling, bones shivering under our skin, fluttering as in prayer, our eyes gleaming—wait for the call.

At last we are happy.

Yitzhak Orpaz was born to a Chasidic family in Zinkov, Soviet Union, in 1923, and emigrated to Pre-State Israel in 1938. Orpaz has published nine books of stories and novellas, six novels, a trilogy, a book of essays, and a collection of poetry. He has received several literary awards, including the Bialik Prize (1986), the Prime Minister's Prize (2004) and the Israel Prize for Life Achievement (2005).

HEBREW LITERATURE SERIES

The Hebrew Literature Series at Dalkey Archive Press makes available major works of Hebrew-language literature in English translation. Featuring exceptional authors at the forefront of Hebrew letters, the series aims to introduce the rich intellectual and aesthetic diversity of contemporary Hebrew writing and culture to English-language readers.

This series is published in collaboration with the Institute for the Translation of Hebrew Literature, at www.ithl.org.il. Thanks are also due to the Office of Cultural Affairs at the Consulate General of Israel, NY, for their support.

MICHAL AJVAZ, *The Golden Age.*
  The Other City.
PIERRE ALBERT-BIROT, *Grabinoulor.*
YUZ ALESHKOVSKY, *Kangaroo.*
FELIPE ALFAU, *Chromos.*
  Locos.
IVAN ÂNGELO, *The Celebration.*
  The Tower of Glass.
ANTÓNIO LOBO ANTUNES, *Knowledge of Hell.*
  The Splendor of Portugal.
ALAIN ARIAS-MISSON, *Theatre of Incest.*
JOHN ASHBERY AND JAMES SCHUYLER,
  A Nest of Ninnies.
ROBERT ASHLEY, *Perfect Lives.*
GABRIELA AVIGUR-ROTEM, *Heatwave*
  and Crazy Birds.
DJUNA BARNES, *Ladies Almanack.*
  Ryder.
JOHN BARTH, *LETTERS.*
  Sabbatical.
DONALD BARTHELME, *The King.*
  Paradise.
SVETISLAV BASARA, *Chinese Letter.*
MIQUEL BAUÇÀ, *The Siege in the Room.*
RENÉ BELLETTO, *Dying.*
MAREK BIEŃCZYK, *Transparency.*
ANDREI BITOV, *Pushkin House.*
ANDREJ BLATNIK, *You Do Understand.*
LOUIS PAUL BOON, *Chapel Road.*
  My Little War.
  Summer in Termuren.
ROGER BOYLAN, *Killoyle.*
IGNÁCIO DE LOYOLA BRANDÃO,
  Anonymous Celebrity.
  Zero.
BONNIE BREMSER, *Troia: Mexican Memoirs.*
CHRISTINE BROOKE-ROSE, *Amalgamemnon.*
BRIGID BROPHY, *In Transit.*
GERALD L. BRUNS, *Modern Poetry and*
  the Idea of Language.
GABRIELLE BURTON, *Heartbreak Hotel.*
MICHEL BUTOR, *Degrees.*
  Mobile.
G. CABRERA INFANTE, *Infante's Inferno.*
  Three Trapped Tigers.
JULIETA CAMPOS,
  The Fear of Losing Eurydice.
ANNE CARSON, *Eros the Bittersweet.*
ORLY CASTEL-BLOOM, *Dolly City.*
LOUIS-FERDINAND CÉLINE, *Castle to Castle.*
  Conversations with Professor Y.
  London Bridge.
  Normance.
  North.
  Rigadoon.
MARIE CHAIX, *The Laurels of Lake Constance.*
HUGO CHARTERIS, *The Tide Is Right.*
ERIC CHEVILLARD, *Demolishing Nisard.*
MARC CHOLODENKO, *Mordechai Schamz.*
JOSHUA COHEN, *Witz.*
EMILY HOLMES COLEMAN, *The Shutter*
  of Snow.
ROBERT COOVER, *A Night at the Movies.*
STANLEY CRAWFORD, *Log of the S.S. The*
  Mrs Unguentine.
  Some Instructions to My Wife.
RENÉ CREVEL, *Putting My Foot in It.*
RALPH CUSACK, *Cadenza.*
NICHOLAS DELBANCO, *The Count of Concord.*
  Sherbrookes.
NIGEL DENNIS, *Cards of Identity.*

PETER DIMOCK, *A Short Rhetoric for*
  Leaving the Family.
ARIEL DORFMAN, *Konfidenz.*
COLEMAN DOWELL,
  Island People.
  Too Much Flesh and Jabez.
ARKADII DRAGOMOSHCHENKO, *Dust.*
RIKKI DUCORNET, *The Complete*
  Butcher's Tales.
  The Fountains of Neptune.
  The Jade Cabinet.
  Phosphor in Dreamland.
WILLIAM EASTLAKE, *The Bamboo Bed.*
  Castle Keep.
  Lyric of the Circle Heart.
JEAN ECHENOZ, *Chopin's Move.*
STANLEY ELKIN, *A Bad Man.*
  Criers and Kibitzers, Kibitzers
  and Criers.
  The Dick Gibson Show.
  The Franchiser.
  The Living End.
  Mrs. Ted Bliss.
FRANÇOIS EMMANUEL, *Invitation to a*
  Voyage.
SALVADOR ESPRIU, *Ariadne in the*
  Grotesque Labyrinth.
LESLIE A. FIEDLER, *Love and Death in*
  the American Novel.
JUAN FILLOY, *Op Oloop.*
ANDY FITCH, *Pop Poetics.*
GUSTAVE FLAUBERT, *Bouvard and Pécuchet.*
KASS FLEISHER, *Talking out of School.*
FORD MADOX FORD,
  The March of Literature.
JON FOSSE, *Aliss at the Fire.*
  Melancholy.
MAX FRISCH, *I'm Not Stiller.*
  Man in the Holocene.
CARLOS FUENTES, *Christopher Unborn.*
  Distant Relations.
  Terra Nostra.
  Where the Air Is Clear.
TAKEHIKO FUKUNAGA, *Flowers of Grass.*
WILLIAM GADDIS, *J R.*
  The Recognitions.
JANICE GALLOWAY, *Foreign Parts.*
  The Trick Is to Keep Breathing.
WILLIAM H. GASS, *Cartesian Sonata*
  and Other Novellas.
  Finding a Form.
  A Temple of Texts.
  The Tunnel.
  Willie Masters' Lonesome Wife.
GÉRARD GAVARRY, *Hoppla! 1 2 3.*
ETIENNE GILSON,
  The Arts of the Beautiful.
  Forms and Substances in the Arts.
C. S. GISCOMBE, *Giscome Road.*
  Here.
DOUGLAS GLOVER, *Bad News of the Heart.*
WITOLD GOMBROWICZ,
  A Kind of Testament.
PAULO EMÍLIO SALES GOMES, *P's Three*
  Women.
GEORGI GOSPODINOV, *Natural Novel.*
JUAN GOYTISOLO, *Count Julian.*
  Juan the Landless.
  Makbara.
  Marks of Identity.

SELECTED DALKEY ARCHIVE TITLES

HENRY GREEN, *Back.*
Blindness.
Concluding.
Doting.
Nothing.
JACK GREEN, *Fire the Bastards!*
JIŘÍ GRUŠA, *The Questionnaire.*
MELA HARTWIG, *Am I a Redundant*
Human Being?
JOHN HAWKES, *The Passion Artist.*
Whistlejacket.
ELIZABETH HEIGHWAY, ED., *Contemporary*
Georgian Fiction.
ALEKSANDAR HEMON, ED.,
Best European Fiction.
AIDAN HIGGINS, *Balcony of Europe.*
Blind Man's Bluff
Bornholm Night-Ferry.
Flotsam and Jetsam.
Langrishe, Go Down.
Scenes from a Receding Past.
KEIZO HINO, *Isle of Dreams.*
KAZUSHI HOSAKA, *Plainsong.*
ALDOUS HUXLEY, *Antic Hay.*
Crome Yellow.
Point Counter Point.
Those Barren Leaves.
Time Must Have a Stop.
NAOYUKI II, *The Shadow of a Blue Cat.*
GERT JONKE, *The Distant Sound.*
Geometric Regional Novel.
Homage to Czerny.
The System of Vienna.
JACQUES JOUET, *Mountain R.*
Savage.
Upstaged.
MIEKO KANAI, *The Word Book.*
YORAM KANIUK, *Life on Sandpaper.*
HUGH KENNER, *Flaubert.*
Joyce and Beckett: The Stoic Comedians.
Joyce's Voices.
DANILO KIŠ, *The Attic.*
Garden, Ashes.
The Lute and the Scars
Psalm 44.
A Tomb for Boris Davidovich.
ANITA KONKKA, *A Fool's Paradise.*
GEORGE KONRÁD, *The City Builder.*
TADEUSZ KONWICKI, *A Minor Apocalypse.*
The Polish Complex.
MENIS KOUMANDAREAS, *Koula.*
ELAINE KRAF, *The Princess of 72nd Street.*
JIM KRUSOE, *Iceland.*
AYŞE KULIN, *Farewell: A Mansion in*
Occupied Istanbul.
EMILIO LASCANO TEGUI, *On Elegance*
While Sleeping.
ERIC LAURRENT, *Do Not Touch.*
VIOLETTE LEDUC, *La Bâtarde.*
EDOUARD LEVÉ, *Autoportrait.*
Suicide.
MARIO LEVI, *Istanbul Was a Fairy Tale.*
DEBORAH LEVY, *Billy and Girl.*
JOSÉ LEZAMA LIMA, *Paradiso.*
ROSA LIKSOM, *Dark Paradise.*
OSMAN LINS, *Avalovara.*
The Queen of the Prisons of Greece.
ALF MAC LOCHLAINN,
The Corpus in the Library.
Out of Focus.
RON LOEWINSOHN, *Magnetic Field(s).*
MINA LOY, *Stories and Essays of Mina Loy.*

D. KEITH MANO, *Take Five.*
MICHELINE AHARONIAN MARCOM,
The Mirror in the Well.
BEN MARCUS,
The Age of Wire and String.
WALLACE MARKFIELD,
Teitlebaum's Window.
To an Early Grave.
DAVID MARKSON, *Reader's Block.*
Wittgenstein's Mistress.
CAROLE MASO, *AVA.*
LADISLAV MATEJKA AND KRYSTYNA
POMORSKA, EDS.,
Readings in Russian Poetics:
Formalist and Structuralist Views.
HARRY MATHEWS, *Cigarettes.*
The Conversions.
The Human Country: New and
Collected Stories.
The Journalist.
My Life in CIA.
Singular Pleasures.
The Sinking of the Odradek
Stadium.
Tlooth.
JOSEPH MCELROY,
Night Soul and Other Stories.
ABDELWAHAB MEDDEB, *Talismano.*
GERHARD MEIER, *Isle of the Dead.*
HERMAN MELVILLE, *The Confidence-Man.*
AMANDA MICHALOPOULOU, *I'd Like.*
STEVEN MILLHAUSER, *The Barnum Museum.*
In the Penny Arcade.
RALPH J. MILLS, JR., *Essays on Poetry.*
MOMUS, *The Book of Jokes.*
CHRISTINE MONTALBETTI, *The Origin of Man.*
Western.
OLIVE MOORE, *Spleen.*
NICHOLAS MOSLEY, *Accident.*
Assassins.
Catastrophe Practice.
Experience and Religion.
A Garden of Trees.
Hopeful Monsters.
Imago Bird.
Impossible Object.
Inventing God.
Judith.
Look at the Dark.
Natalie Natalia.
Serpent.
Time at War.
WARREN MOTTE,
Fables of the Novel: French Fiction
since 1990.
Fiction Now: The French Novel in
the 21st Century.
Oulipo: A Primer of Potential
Literature.
GERALD MURNANE, *Barley Patch.*
Inland.
YVES NAVARRE, *Our Share of Time.*
Sweet Tooth.
DOROTHY NELSON, *In Night's City.*
Tar and Feathers.
ESHKOL NEVO, *Homesick.*
WILFRIDO D. NOLLEDO, *But for the Lovers.*
FLANN O'BRIEN, *At Swim-Two-Birds.*
The Best of Myles.
The Dalkey Archive.
The Hard Life.
The Poor Mouth.

FOR A FULL LIST OF PUBLICATIONS, VISIT:
www.dalkeyarchive.com

SELECTED DALKEY ARCHIVE TITLES

DUMITRU TSEPENEAG, *Hotel Europa.*
　The Necessary Marriage.
　Pigeon Post.
　Vain Art of the Fugue.
ESTHER TUSQUETS, *Stranded.*
DUBRAVKA UGRESIC, *Lend Me Your Character.*
　Thank You for Not Reading.
TOR ULVEN, *Replacement.*
MATI UNT, *Brecht at Night.*
　Diary of a Blood Donor.
　Things in the Night.
ÁLVARO URIBE AND OLIVIA SEARS, EDS.,
　Best of Contemporary Mexican Fiction.
ELOY URROZ, *Friction.*
　The Obstacles.
LUISA VALENZUELA, *Dark Desires and
　the Others.*
　He Who Searches.
PAUL VERHAEGHEN, *Omega Minor.*
AGLAJA VETERANYI, *Why the Child Is
　Cooking in the Polenta.*
BORIS VIAN, *Heartsnatcher.*
LLORENÇ VILLALONGA, *The Dolls' Room.*
TOOMAS VINT, *An Unending Landscape.*
ORNELA VORPSI, *The Country Where No
　One Ever Dies.*
AUSTRYN WAINHOUSE, *Hedyphagetica.*
CURTIS WHITE, *America's Magic Mountain.*
　The Idea of Home.
　Memories of My Father Watching TV.
　Requiem.

DIANE WILLIAMS, *Excitability:
　Selected Stories.*
　Romancer Erector.
DOUGLAS WOOLF, *Wall to Wall.*
　Ya! & John-Juan.
JAY WRIGHT, *Polynomials and Pollen.*
　*The Presentable Art of Reading
　Absence.*
PHILIP WYLIE, *Generation of Vipers.*
MARGUERITE YOUNG, *Angel in the Forest.*
　Miss MacIntosh, My Darling.
REYOUNG, *Unbabbling.*
VLADO ŽABOT, *The Succubus.*
ZORAN ŽIVKOVIĆ, *Hidden Camera.*
LOUIS ZUKOFSKY, *Collected Fiction.*
VITOMIL ZUPAN, *Minuet for Guitar.*
SCOTT ZWIREN, *God Head.*